# LOUDER
## THAN WORDS

### ASHLEY WOODFOLK &
### LEXI UNDERWOOD

SCHOLASTIC PRESS / NEW YORK

Library of Congress Cataloging-in-Publication Data available

ISBN 978-1-338-87557-7

10 9 8 7 6 5 4 3 2 1          24 25 26 27 28

Printed in the U.S.A.          37

First edition, June 2024

Book design by Stephanie Yang

TO THOSE WHO WORRY THEY'VE
DONE UNFORGIVABLE THINGS:
THERE IS STILL HOPE

# PART ONE
# SEPTEMBER

# 1

First days have a way of making me feel a little less than real.

The way no one looks too long at me, but everyone looks for a second longer than feels comfortable. The way I can pass through the hallways like a ghost but still stick out like a thorny rose in a field of wispy wildflowers. The way I don't speak, sometimes for hours, until I'm forced to, and my voice comes out all croaky. I sound nothing like myself, but no one knows that I sound nothing like myself. Because no one knows me.

In a way, feeling less than real is good. I like feeling like an outline or an early version of one of my sketches: still flat and gray and waiting to be made whole. And if I'm not real—if there are no expectations about how I'm supposed to look or act or sound—I can be whomever I want.

This is a second chance, and second chances are rare. I may not deserve this opportunity for a fresh start, but I need to do something right to make up for all the wrong. So here I'll be someone different. Someone good. A better person than I was before.

The concrete stairs leading up to the front doors of Edgewood High are narrow and steep, and late-summer sunlight filters through the branches of two tall oaks springing up like giants on either side of the entrance. I want to sit in the grass and trace the way the light dapples the school's stoop in uneven shapes, take stock of the shadows and the few leaves that have already turned and fallen, though it's still much too warm to be autumn. This part of DC is so different from the section of the city where my old school was—the houses are smaller, the bus stops and Metro stations busier and louder—and I want to document that too, how much more this school feels like it's inside the version of the city I know. But I wasted enough time deciding what to wear this morning and I don't want to be late. I hike my backpack higher on my shoulders and pull open one of the school's double doors, trying hard not to think about the reason I'm here.

Conversations swell and subside all around as I step into the wide entryway. Kids in mint-green T-shirts and tangerine shorts, violet tank tops and bright yellow sneakers fill my sightline with color, and it's a jarring reminder that I'm in public school now. Hartwell Academy, my old private school, was so stuffy and obsessed with tradition that we all had to wear a bland navy-and-white uniform that almost made me forget how much I love putting together a look. As I glance around at students with blue braids and funky shoelaces, I see that even some of the teachers have several piercings in a single ear or are wearing glittery makeup. My handmade jewelry doesn't seem so out of place in a school like this one. And neither do I, I realize, noticing how many faces are various shades of brown. Unlike the whitewashed halls of Hartwell, so many more people here look like me.

Unconsciously, I touch my laid edges, the puff pulled tight at the crown of my head. I look down to see if I need to straighten the collar of my oversize flannel or retie my spotless white Chucks. I don't, and I smile, grateful that I at least *look* perfect.

I'm so used to being different and doing everything I can to adapt to everything and everyone around me. It hadn't occurred to me that here I might be able to blend in. That I might even *fit* in. I feel my heart speed up, stutter, skip a beat. It's a sure sign that I'm nervous—and the only remaining sign that my heart has ever struggled to do what it's supposed to. The painless arrhythmia also makes me miss an old friend, Bree. When I felt the stutter with her, it was usually from excitement. I decide to assign that emotion to this moment instead of anxiety, hoping the stutter is a sign of good things to come and not a warning, as it sometimes can be.

According to my schedule, the room number of my first class is A450, but after walking around for ten minutes without success-fully finding *any* rooms that start with the letter A, hiking up and back down a flight of stairs, and getting so turned around I pass the same water fountain three times, I realize I won't figure this out on my own and decide to look for the office.

Hartwell was tiny compared to Edgewood's long hallways, its dozens of hidden corridors and towering flights of stairs. I go down one hall and then another, turning right and heading toward what I think might be the main office, but as I come around the corner, I slam right into a statuesque Black girl with a bleached-blond buzz cut and perfectly winged eyeliner.

"Oh God, I'm so sorry," I say immediately. She bends down to pick up a composition notebook and her phone, which flew out of her hand when we collided. "I'm new and I'm all turned around. I can't find the office and I thought it was around here some-where, but—"

"You good," she says. "I'm Scarlett, and I'm a little turned around too. I'm ... well ... newish. But yeah, I just left the office." She throws a thumb over her shoulder, pointing to a dark blue door, and smiles.

I let out a relieved sigh. "Right. Thanks. Your phone okay?"

She nods. "Phone's cool," she says, holding it up so I can see that the screen isn't scratched or cracked.

"Oh, perfect. I'm Jordyn," I tell her, reaching out for a handshake.

The girl looks at my outstretched hand and then back up at my face, squinting. For a second, I swear I see a flicker of recognition in her eyes, but where could this girl possibly know me from? The moment passes as quickly as it came, but her smile fades.

When she doesn't reach for my hand, I let it fall.

"Are you a junior too?" I ask. "It would be a relief to know at least one person. Maybe we have some classes together?"

Scarlett shrugs and fiddles with one of the studs in her ear. "Maybe," she says. Then she walks away without looking back, her round, blond head floating a few inches above most of the other students'.

For a moment I'm embarrassed by the way she brushed me off— by how little she seemed to want to know me. But then I remember that I want this year to be different. The old Jordyn would over- think this situation and wonder if there was something she did wrong, something about her that turned Scarlett off. But I'm the

New Jordyn now. I head to the office, telling myself to let Scarlett's rejection roll off my shoulders like rain, but her rejection lingers overhead like a storm cloud.

The admin assistant in the office is instantly able to point me in the right direction for first period, so I stumble into Mr. Roderick's Digital Design class just before the bell sounds—a flat tone that reverberates against the concrete walls and makes my ears ring in a way that means I'll be hearing it tonight in my dreams. "Jesus," I mutter under my breath as I walk in, and I earn a half grin from a curly-haired white boy sitting in the front row.

"I know," he says. "It takes some getting used to, and then it's still terrible."

I can't help but smile. I glance around and I'm surprised to see Scarlett in the class too, seated right in the middle. I don't want to have to walk past her and relive whatever her icy reaction to me in the hall was about, so I take the empty seat beside the boy. "My old school didn't have bells—swore they were disruptive to the *retention of information* and the *facilitation of deep discussion*," I say, and he chuckles.

"I'm Jordyn," I add, taking a risk old Jordyn would never have taken again so soon after being brushed off by Scarlett. But New Jordyn dives right in. "This room was, like, impossible to find."

"Kaleb," he says. There's a tiny, sparkling stud in his nose, shining like a fleck of glitter when he turns his head. "And yeah. We call this part of the building the Attic because it's so far away from everything."

"Is that what the weird *A* stands for?" I ask.

Kaleb laughs and tucks one of his curls behind his ear. "I think it actually stands for *annex*? But sure, let's say that it does. Roderick is def weird enough to live in one."

I glance up at our teacher. He's stocky and tan, with salt-and-pepper hair and a sky-colored shirt he has buttoned all the way to the top. He's handsome in a nerdy way, like an actor playing a college professor, or a scientist who works out.

"What's weird about him?" I ask, and Kaleb just shakes his head.

"You'll see," he says.

"Okay!" Mr. Roderick says seconds later. He pushes his gray hair away from his gray eyes and slips on a pair of horn-rimmed glasses, completing his look in a way I approve of. *How could someone as stylish as him be anything but cool?* I think, glancing over at Kaleb.

"Let's get started," the teacher says.

He reviews the syllabus with us and tells us what software we'll be using in class as well as the projects we'll be required to complete in order to put our new design skills into practice. At first, I think

Kaleb is completely wrong about Mr. Roderick, and I'm interested in almost everything he mentions. Though I still love drawing by hand, graphic design is really fun for me too, and I know those are skills that I'll need if I'm going to get into a good art school. But then I notice how Roderick glances at a cute Asian girl in the front row as he says that some students have a *natural* talent with the software, while others (did he just look at *me*?) don't.

When he moves on to how we'll be working in groups the first semester to make sample zines, I start getting excited again. I tell myself I must be imagining things, until he starts sharing examples of what subject matter our zines can cover. "Your group's zine can be about whatever subject you like. Reviews of the best ethnic restaurants in your neighborhood; basketball, movie, or book ratings; queer rights; feminism . . ." He gestures, actually *gestures*, to an Indian student when he says the thing about ethnic restaurants, to a Black kid when he mentions basketball, and then in Kaleb's direction when he says the word *queer*.

I stretch my eyes at Kaleb. Is this guy serious? "Uhhh," Kaleb says. But he doesn't continue, just shakes his head and whispers, "Wow."

About halfway through class, Kaleb fashions a tiny flag out of notebook paper and writes the word *RED* on its tiny mast. Then he holds it up facing me every time Mr. Roderick says or does something problematic...which definitely happens more often than it should. It makes me feel like my skin is a beacon, shining and brown, and I'm anxious and unsettled waiting for him to say or do something particularly awful to me. Kaleb's flag is a salve, making me snort because of his impeccable comedic timing, but after three or four moments that make me increasingly uncomfortable, I'm wondering how the rest of the class is feeling—if anyone else's skin feels too tight, or like it's a target waiting to be Roderick's bull's-eye. I think something needs to be said, but I'm not sure if I should be the one to say it. Roderick's jokes are always just shy of offensive, his comments on the verge of being mean but just subtle enough to be denied—the micro-est microaggressions. I've had teachers like him before, but it was worse at Hartwell, where my face was often the only one with color in any given classroom. I felt alone or like I was the only one who noticed. Here things feel different—*are* different—I remind myself, glancing over at Kaleb. And I'm different now too.

But I don't cancel Roderick just yet. I let his BS slide since it's the first day, hoping that he's nervous being in front of a new group of students he doesn't know or that I'm being extra sensitive since I'm in a new place. Still, it's a comfort that Kaleb sees his messiness too. At least I know I'm not the only one.

"Wow," I whisper as I pack my bag at the end of class. "You weren't kidding."

Kaleb raises his eyebrows. "Tip of the iceberg, J. Tippy top of the iceberg."

I smile a little at his use of a nickname even though we just met. But I guess we did kinda bond over the last forty minutes. "Sooo, now that we've survived *that* guy, you got any other classes in the Attic?" I ask as we step out of Roderick's classroom and into the hall. Kaleb smirks.

"I was about to ask you the same thing," he says.

I like this kid's vibe. Plus, the way he read Mr. Roderick right away makes me want to keep him close.

"I'm pretty sure I do," Kaleb continues. He pulls up his schedule on his phone and shows it to me. I pull up mine to compare it with his. "We have two other classes together," I say, trying to contain my excitement, wondering if I've already made my first friend.

"Nice," he says. His phone vibrates in his hand, a text notification appearing, and I glance at it by accident:

Mila: *Seen the new girl yet? She cute?*

This Mila person, whoever she is, couldn't mean me . . . could she?

Kaleb clicks the power button, putting his phone to sleep. I can't tell if he knows that I saw. His nails are painted a sparkling shade of blue, and I ask him the name of the color, just so he doesn't feel the need to address the text if he doesn't want to. "Dark Side of the Moon," he says, wiggling his fingers so his nails shimmer. Then he asks me about my bracelets, my flannel, the earrings I'm wearing that I made this weekend. He loves it all, and I blush, hoping he likes me as much as my accessories.

"Guess I'll be seeing you soon," he says as the warning bell rings. As he turns to leave, he adds, "Mila loves gossip. Don't worry about her."

I smile and nod.

I can tell that Kaleb is *good*. Kind and open and real. It's only my first day, but I feel like he's someone I want on my side—exactly the kind of person the new me needs.

"See ya," I say, feeling the new girl loneliness close around me like fog the farther away he gets.

———

Navigating the rest of the morning is fairly easy, once I know where the Attic is. My other classes are closer together, and while I don't connect with any other students the way I did with Kaleb, when it's time for lunch, I'm not feeling too bad. The cafeteria is big and crowded, and people are laughing and tossing french fries like they do in the movies. Freshmen carry trays and look a little bit lost, but everyone else already seems to have a place they belong—a fact that makes my chest feel kind of tight, my face a little hot. But knowing I'll see Kaleb again in the afternoon makes me feel better.

I eat in a quiet corner at a mostly empty table and read on my phone, too intimidated by the wide-open room to approach any of the kids sitting and talking together. It makes me ache a little for the friends I had at my old school, but then I remind myself of the things they said, the terrible things we did. I ache a little for Bree too, despite the turn our friendship took. But I can't afford to forget the way it all ended, how difficult the summer was, the way I felt like I wouldn't survive. Today is hard, but I know that eventually things will be better here. They have to be.

---

"You're Jordyn, right?"

In my next three classes, I hear this half a dozen times. Either that or, "So, *you're* Jordyn," though I know for a fact that Kaleb and Scarlett are the only two humans I've uttered my name to since I stepped foot in this building. Somehow many more people than that know who I am. Eyes follow me in the halls, and it seems like the other kids are glancing over their shoulders at me, whispering with their friends while looking in my direction. And then there are the ones who look down their nose at me, who give me a wide berth, the students, like Scarlett, who rebuff my attempts at friendliness. The lack of introductions I get to make are reminders of Mila's text, and what Kaleb said about gossip. But I still don't get it. I haven't been here long enough to be the subject of rumors, and even if I had been a student here last year, we haven't even gotten through a full day of school yet. Fear about what it all could mean makes my hands go clammy, so I keep rubbing them down my thighs and shoving them deep into my pockets.

The next time I see Kaleb, I say, "Yo . . . How does everyone know me?" Kaleb laughs and shrugs. "Word travels fast when you're a new kid, I guess."

"This seems like more than just being new," I tell him, looking around nervously. He doesn't seem that worried, just laughs again, acknowledges that it's annoying but promises that it will die down, that I'm just a shiny new toy. But I need to know what's going on. Truth be told, I'm a little afraid that I won't like whatever I find out.

The answer doesn't come until I finally get the guts to ask someone else about it in my last class.

"You're Jordyn, right?" a curvy girl with dark wavy hair asks as soon as I walk into Physics, before I even have a chance to let my bag slide off my shoulder.

"Uh, yeah?" I say. "That's me. But . . ." I glance around and step closer to her before I whisper, "How does everyone already know my name?"

The girl lowers her voice too. "Oh, *everyone* has been talking about you, Jordyn Jones. The newbie from private school. You're shorter than I thought you'd be though. Anyway, they've been saying you're not talking to anyone because you think you're better than us, but I was like, chill, she's new. She could just be nervous!"

I smile, appreciating her kindness, though I'm unnerved that she knows even more than just my name. Hartwell Academy is home to the kids of diplomats and senators—big-time lobbyists, journalists, and other politicians who all work on Capitol Hill. It doesn't surprise me that people who know I went there might think I'm stuck up.

"It's definitely more the nervousness than anything," I say. "But I still don't get it. How do you know I went to private school?"

"Oh," she says, sounding surprised. "Kaleb didn't tell you?"

The skin on the back of my neck prickles. "You're . . . friends with Kaleb?" I ask.

"Yeah, hi! I'm Mila. I thought he would have told you."

"Told me what?" I swallow hard, hoping my instinct about Kaleb wasn't wrong.

Mila smiles an easy smile and touches my arm. A dimple pops into her left cheek. "I didn't mean to freak you out! Just thought he would have told you about Tomcat Tea. It's our school's podcast. Someone started it during lockdown and it got super popular because we were all bored a.f. at home doing virtual school." She faux gags. "Whoever runs it set up this email address where people can send in tips and gossip, and they put it all into a weekly show. Maybe someone sent in a tip about you."

She pauses for a second, and I take the moment to process what she's just told me: podcast, anonymous tips, me. Mila taps her nails on her bottom lip before she speaks again. "I guess Kaleb wouldn't have told you about it, actually. He kinda hates the pod and probably hasn't listened to the newest episode." She grins again.

"A podcast, huh?"

"Yep," Mila says. She reaches into her pocket and pulls out a tube of lipstick, turning her mouth a pale shade of peach. It's a beautiful contrast against her light brown skin, and I finally smile back.

"I hope it's mostly good things?" I say.

Mila makes a face that's somewhere between a wince and an awkward smile, and moves her hands around like she's looking for the right words. I like how expressive she is—how she talks with her whole body and how her face hides nothing. "It's mostly . . . things," she says. "You should listen though, so at least you'll know what they're saying about you. Here, gimme your phone."

I pull it from my pocket and watch as she taps around my screen, showing me where I can stream it. She hits subscribe for me too, so I'll always know when a new episode drops.

"They?" I ask. "Don't tell me there's more than one person I have to worry about."

Mila shakes her head and her big silver hoops swing under her hair. "They, singular. No one knows who the podcaster is. It's a whole thing." She hands my phone back before tilting her head at me for a second. "You're cute," Mila says. "We should hang out. Kaleb said you were cool too."

I look down, blushing a little. "Well, whatever's on that podcast must not be that bad if you wanna chill with me."

"I didn't say all *that*," she teases as the teacher comes into class and tells us all to sit and quiet down. "But what can I say, Private School? I'm a sucker for a pretty face, even if it means trouble."

Hello, fellow students! We're back! Did you miss me? You know how much I missed you. I couldn't be more excited because we have a lot of tea to spill. Last season showed just how messy the people we go to school with can be, so it would be cruel of me not to give you all the sordid details. Let's buckle up for a wild school year.

Now, let's get into it: Over the summer, the power couple we thought would be together forever, Cassie Taylor and Devon Wheeler, sadly broke up while audibly sobbing at the Smoothie King at the mall. Eyewitness reports say it was a, quote, "tough watch." Considering we expected them to be prom queen and king this year, this bumps up Bella Martins's and Luke Haley's chances of winning. If they make it till then, that is. Also, believe it or not, Chance Martinez, who up to now was best known for attempting a backflip in his mascot costume and having the head fly off, went viral over break and has become an internet sensation on TikTok. In case you were lucky enough to miss it, his newfound stardom . . . is from posting thirst traps. The internet really is an *interesting* place.

And for our new students—a special welcome to all our freshmen! Heads up, *High School Musical* lied. Have low expectations.

Speaking of freshmen, does everyone remember that one girl who left suddenly before sophomore year? Good ol' Scarlett Fisher. Well, rumor has it she'll be back and gracing the junior hallways this year. You may be asking, "Why bring up Scarlett?" Well, I honestly am a little suspicious of her return. The real question is, why didn't she tell anyone she was leaving, and more importantly, why is she coming back?

Scarlett isn't the only newcomer to the junior class: A Miss Jordyn Jones will be making her arrival at Edgewood. Apparently Jordyn is joining us fresh off an expulsion! Not to mention this is her first time in a public school. I guess the princess turned into a frog, whomp whomp. But for what reason? What could little Miss Jones do that was so bad her old school expelled her? Don't worry, what's done in the dark comes to light. And the moment it does, I'll make sure to be the first one to let you all know.

And finally, for the last segment of this episode, we have everybody's favorite: BOMBSHELL, where we drop some tea so piping hot that it'll leave you craving the next episode. This week's star is . . . Jasmine Everett! Jasmine, we've heard that over the summer you may or may not have had not a boob or a nose job, but *toe-shortening surgery* . . . By the looks of her feet in those Gucci slides today, the rumors seem to be true. Guess all those LaCienega Boulevardez jokes got to her. Either way, you look great, girl. If only everyone had a rich daddy who could magically fix our problems.

With that, happy start of a new school year and start of another beautiful season of Tomcat Tea. I'll be back next episode with more tea. Stay tuned, and stay messy. Let's go, Tomcats!

# 2

"So . . ." my mom says the second I walk through the front door. "How was it?"

I listened to Tomcat Tea on the ride home from school while I sketched a passenger sitting across from me on the bus, and I'm still processing everything the host somehow knew about me. The way my heart stuttered and skipped as I listened let me know the words were landing harder than I was willing to admit.

The podcaster's voice was breathy and gruff, though I don't know if it was a natural huskiness or one that was put on to disguise, and they spoke quickly, enthusiastically—their tone cheerful, like they enjoy wreaking havoc with gossip every week. When the podcast got too stressful to keep drawing, my heart feeling like it was doing jumping jacks in my chest, I watched the street names pass in alphabetical order—Franklin, Girard, Hamlin, Irving—until my bus curved around Seventh Street, crossing Michigan Avenue and delivering me home.

I take off my backpack and stare down at my phone. Who is this podcaster? How did they know my name and about my expulsion? I wanted this to be a fresh start. A chance to be someone new. How can I do that with someone blurting out stuff about me—and my past—to the whole school? Do they know anything else about me and my friends from Hartwell? And if so, when or who might they tell? I think about Kaleb's kind eyes and his quick grin, Mila's warm, reassuring hand on my shoulder. Their funny nicknames for me.

I can't let this podcast ruin my chance to start over.

"Earth to Jordyn," my mom says, snapping me out of my head. I blink a few times and look up at her. She's wearing a jumpsuit in her favorite color—bloodred—and she must have just gotten home because she still has on matching crimson lipstick. It briefly reminds me of Scarlett, and I suddenly wonder if her reaction to me was related to the podcast. Mom makes it a point to make it home before I do every day—has since I first started school. She's an art dealer, so I get my love of drawing and flair for fashion from her, but even when she has an evening gallery opening to attend, she makes sure not to head out until after she checks in with me when I get home from school.

"Oh, hey, Mom. It was a little weird. Kinda lonely. But okay."

She nods and unties the patterned headwrap holding up her locs, letting them tumble down her back. Then she washes her hands and lifts the kettle from the stove. She beckons me forward, into the kitchen, and when I sit down in our little breakfast nook, she slides me a cup of tea the way she does every afternoon. It's warm and milky, just the way I like it. When Mom's in a jokey mood, she'll say, "One light-skinned tea for my light-skinned child," but this afternoon she just says, "That will get better with time, boo. The loneliness. You'll make new friends. *Better* friends."

I sip my tea and try to think about Mila and Kaleb instead of the podcast. "Yeah, I hope so. When's Daddy getting home from the restaurant?"

She grins. "He said he'd be back late tonight, so since he won't be here to cook or bring us leftovers, we're ordering Thai."

I grin wide. "Yesssss," I say. The only food I like more than my daddy's is Thai. And since he loves trying out new recipes for his soul food restaurant, Bread & Butter, on his family before adding them to the menu, we usually only order in on the weekends when

B&B is busiest. "You must feel pretty bad for me if we're ordering in on a Monday."

"You deserve it, sweetheart. I know it's hard to start over your junior year, but I'm so proud of you for wanting to make a change. I think Edgewood is going to be just what you need after last year. Just what we all need."

I don't tell her about Tomcat Tea—what the host knows. What they've already shared. I don't know how deep the rabbit hole goes or if there is an end to their knowledge. I can't begin to imagine who might be their source.

I smile at my mom and tell her I think she's right. When she stands to put the kettle back on the stove, I take out my phone. Mila texted me on the way home. She'd sent herself a message from my phone when she'd saved my number. Her message to me just said, *Did you listen?* Now I text her back.

*I did. I don't know how I feel about it. This person is really anon? No one has any idea who it is?*

*Nope*, she sends back. *But it's harmless.*

*I don't know. I have a bad feeling about it. People with that kind of power usually can't be trusted.*

*Whoa, Private School. I really don't think it's that serious. Besides, by next week the pod will be about something and someone else.*

I don't text back for a beat, nibbling on my bottom lip and wondering if she's right. Wondering if she's going to ask why I got expelled from my last school.

*I guess I just don't like someone else telling people who they think I am.*

When Mila doesn't text right back, I look up at my mom.

I start speaking slowly. I don't want to tell my mom everything, but I need her advice. "Since this is supposed to be my chance to start again, I want to do things right."

She nods, sitting back down at the table. "I know you do, honey."

"So, like, what do I do if people are talking about me? I think it's just the whole being-the-new-girl thing, but I don't want it to get out of hand. I don't want people forming an opinion about me before they even know who I am."

My mom grips her mug for a second, then she reaches across the space between us and places her fingers over the knuckles of the hand I have resting on the table. Her palm is hot to the touch. "You can't control other people, Jordyn. What they say or what they do. All you can control is yourself. You can show people who you are, and, as they say, actions are much louder than words. *Your* actions can be louder than *their* words. Show people who you are, again and again if you must, and they'll believe what they see more than any rumor they hear."

"I didn't say anything about rumors," I mutter, pulling my hand from beneath hers and picking up my phone again. Mila has texted back, *Oh, I get it, boo. But not gonna lie, the pod stats about you def intrigued me.* ☺. I smile, feeling the icy ache of anxiety melt a little at Mila's text and my mother's words. Both make me feel powerful.

"You're a survivor," my mother adds. "Always have been. You'll be fine."

I smile and scoot closer to my mom, knowing she's thinking about me as a tiny infant with a sick heart; as a toddler who missed milestones; as a kid who was always small for her age even as I caught up to other kids in every other way. But she doesn't bring it up, so I don't either. I just switch apps and pull up the menu of our favorite Thai place so we can both see. Then I order enough pad see ew and crab rangoon to feed both versions of myself: the Jordyn from before who was always a victim, and the New Jordyn, me now, who won't be taken advantage of again.

———

During Mr. Roderick's lecture the next day, Kaleb passes me a note.

*Mila told me about Tomcat Tea. I hadn't listened yet. Sry I didn't say anything. I didn't know.*

I scribble a quick one back. *It's cool. Just thought you hated me for a second.*

He makes an exaggerated shocked face, with his hand over his heart. Then he writes, *I could never.*

I smile and jot down: *JK. Mila told me you don't really like the pod.*

*Understatement.* He replies by mouthing the word in my direction.

Today Mr. Roderick is using a slideshow for his lecture. I take notes and pay close attention to everything, determined to do well in this class despite my misgivings about him. Kaleb has his miniature red flag ready for action, but we're more than halfway through class and he hasn't used it at all. I'm chalking up yesterday's weirdness as a fluke when it happens.

Mr. Roderick clicks to the next slide and the screen fills with the face of a Black woman, squinting and looking confused. Roderick narrates, saying, "Now, if you find yourself looking at your screen like this, it could mean you're just not getting it." He mimics the woman's facial expressions, and a few kids in class laugh. The next slide is an image of a Black man, looking similarly lost, and Roderick walks across the room pointing to different kids who he says are making the same kinds of faces. Kaleb slowly lifts his flag.

A third slide follows, featuring yet another Black person, this one a woman making sassy gestures, like she's busy and doesn't have time to answer questions, doesn't have time to deal with the two people on the previous slides who seem to need help. And when Mr.

Roderick puts his hand on his hip and snaps his fingers, I feel this deep ache in the pit of my stomach. I'm so shocked I can't move. But Kaleb does.

He barks out a dark laugh. "I'm sorry, Mr. Roderick, but that is so not okay," Kaleb says. Half the class turns to look at Kaleb and the other half lets out a low "Oooooh . . ." One Black girl sitting across from me says, "Oop!"

Roderick drops his hand from his hip and stops gesticulating. He glares at Kaleb. "You have something to say, Kaleb?"

Kaleb leans forward in his seat. "I'm just really confused. And kinda mad, to be honest. You can't possibly think doing what you're doing is actually funny."

Mr. Roderick looks around at the class. Some kids look away. Some look excited. Some are covering their mouths, their eyes stretched wide. When I glance over at Scarlett, she looks pissed, but that's normal for her. Some kids are actually laughing, but not at Roderick's performance.

"I heard some of your classmates laughing. So maybe you're the one with the problem, Kaleb. Maybe you just have no sense of humor."

Kaleb runs his hands over his face. "This is exactly why I didn't want to take this class. I knew I'd get into it with you from the stories I'd heard. But I'll be honest, I didn't think it would happen this fast."

"Stories?" Roderick says. "What stories?"

Kaleb shakes his head. "Look, it doesn't matter. What does matter is you using digital Blackface in a class about digital design. You, with your hand on your hip imitating a Black woman because you think it's funny."

"*Blackface?*" Roderick is completely stunned. He laughs an uncomfortable, awkward laugh and blinks half a dozen times in a row. "I don't know what you're talking about, and you know what? I don't like your tone. Get your things. You can spend the rest of the class period in the office."

Kaleb scoffs, and I do too, unconsciously—it just happens. Kaleb stands up and starts packing his bag, but his face is all red and blotchy. I can't tell if he's embarrassed, angry, or both, but I know I have a choice to make. Old Jordyn might have stayed quiet, intent on not making waves. And for a second, I feel the old fear of embarrassment, fear of authority, fear of being different or standing out rise in me like a tide. But I *am* different, and I'm finally trying to be okay with that. I shove the fear away, though some of it stays, spilling like water, attempting to flood my bravery. Still, with trembling hands, I stand up.

Kaleb looks over at me like he's surprised I'm standing beside him—surprised I have this kind of fight in me. But we just met, and he doesn't know who I am or who I want to be. He doesn't know what I've done or what to expect of me. And neither does anyone who listened to the podcast, despite what they think they know. I remember all the people who said, "So *you're* Jordyn" yesterday, like they knew something about me. I'm glad I have the opportunity to *show* everyone who I am, like my mom said.

I meet Kaleb's gaze and he smirks, something like realization overtaking his features. *Oh*, I can see him thinking. *Oh, this girl gets it.* And I do. I give him a small nod, and it emboldens him. It emboldens me too.

"You can't just do that," I say. "You can't just send him to the office because you don't like what he has to say. He's right. People like to wear Blackness as a costume all the time, but we're not a joke. We're not here for your entertainment. And where are those same people when the scary stuff happens to us?"

"That's it exactly," Kaleb says. "The same way people like to co-opt queer slang, which also, by the way, usually comes from *Black* queer people."

"Not to mention," I continue, "that it's just kind of awkward to watch you, a white guy, use this photo of a Black woman to make your point. Like, there are a million memes with white people as the subjects. Just pick one of those!"

Roderick looks bored now, like he doesn't care. He's already decided we're wrong, too young, and too angry. I imagine him as one of the old guys quoted in news stories about "today's youth," and then he says exactly what I expect him to. "We get it," he says, sounding sarcastic. "You're *woke* and I'm not. We can go back and forth about this for hours, but what it comes down to is that you don't get the joke. It's fine. Let's agree to disagree."

"No," I hear myself say. "No. It's not an agree-to-disagree thing. You're not listening." I'm getting frustrated. The back of my neck feels hot the way it always feels right before I cry, but I don't want to cry in this class, in front of all these strangers. I don't want to look like an angry Black woman, or like I'm being overly sensitive, or like I'm being dramatic the same way the women in his slideshow are. I need to remain in control. To be calm. To make my point.

So I take a deep breath. I imagine drawing Roderick as a monster and I give him long fangs and thin, gnarled limbs, and make his glasses into huge eyes. People should look on the outside the way they are on the inside, so you know who is safe and who isn't. I draw him in my mind, making him as hideous as his behavior, and I feel my heart rate slowing down, my mind clearing. I'm about to try again to explain why what he's doing is bad, why and whom it hurts—why it's important that he get it. I'm trying to figure out a way to make my points that will penetrate his unwillingness to see. But before I can open my mouth again, Kaleb speaks up:

"The bottom line is, Mr. Roderick, it's low-key racist behavior."

The whole class gasps. But I just think, *Thank you, Kaleb! Thank you!* I'm so glad he said it so I don't have to. I sigh, relieved.

"Excuse me?" Roderick steps closer to Kaleb in a way that feels threatening. "What did you just call me?"

Kaleb doesn't shrink, doesn't back down at all, and I want to hug him. "I didn't call *you* anything. People get so freaking upset by that word and they stop listening to what's actually being said. I didn't call *you* racist, Mr. Roderick, I said that assuming Black personas in the form of memes or GIFs or emojis is a low-key racist *behavior*. You're treating Blackness like a costume. That's why it's called digital *Blackface*. Do you really not get the difference?"

A few kids in the class nod, like they get it, maybe for the first time. A few shake their heads, and I can't tell if they think we're overreacting or if they're shaking their heads at Roderick. But knowing Kaleb gets it is enough for me. I feel supported, backed up, advocated for.

"Yes," I say. "That's it exactly, Kaleb. It's embarrassing and dehumanizing and rude, and how do you, Mr. Roderick, a person who I assume has studied this subject, not get that?"

Now Roderick is the one turning red. The tops of his cheeks are pink, and he balls up his fists at his sides. "Okay, look. You can't disrespect me like this in my own classroom," Roderick says, clearly not having heard Kaleb's clarification or anything I've said at all. He's pissed, when I should be the one who's pissed, and his anger is hard to swallow. "We're done talking about this here, and Jordyn, you can join your new friend in the office. Go ahead, we'll wait."

Kaleb gets a devilish look in his eye and I know he's not done. He's a lit fuse, and there's no stopping him now. He slams his books into his bag, and I pack mine too, hairs on my arms on edge, my whole body feeling hot and shaky.

When we reach the door, Kaleb turns back. His hazel eyes narrow into slits. "You should be teaching us how to avoid being assholes on the internet," he says. He grabs my hand and opens the door. "Not being one yourself."

---

"Detention," Kaleb says. He pretends to rip the pink detention slip in half. "I guess I deserve that."

I laugh, shoving mine into my back pocket. "I mean, maybe? But you were provoked. And not gonna lie, I'd sit in detention for the rest of my life to see his face again when you called him an asshole."

"I didn't call him an asshole," Kaleb insists. "Not directly anyway."

I crack up. "Uh-huh, sure you didn't." The bell rings, loud and indignant, shrill and impossible to ignore. I groan. "Ugh, why is there more school? I hate today. I just wanna go home."

Kaleb pats my arm. "Correct. Today should be canceled, like Roderick. Dislike. Unsubscribe." I pout more, and Kaleb comforts me until we reach the end of the hall.

There, he pushes his dark curls away from his face and says, "Sit with us at lunch today."

"Who's us?" I ask.

"Well, there's me and Mila, and a couple of our other friends. They're cool. You'll like them. They'll love you. Plus, I can't tell the epic-ass story of what happened in first period alone."

I grin and bump his shoulder with mine. "I guess I'll have to abandon my adoring fans to hang out with you guys."

"Jordyn, hate to tell you this, but your books don't count as fans. Or friends."

"Oh, shut up. I'll be there, okay?"

Kaleb smirks. "Cool."

I'm looking for Kaleb when I walk into the cafeteria, but it's Mila who bumps into me right by the door. "Hey," I say. "Kaleb said—"

"Oh, I'm aware. He told me everything. Let's grab some food, then I'll show you where we sit. We need to strategize."

I smile to myself, wondering how they text so much when we're not supposed to use our phones at all in class, but then I see the glossy shine of Mila's smartwatch and I can imagine Kaleb sending her long text stories while he walks between classes; I can see her catching up by just glancing down at her wrist. I follow Mila to the lunch line, filing in behind her as she smiles at the lunch ladies and grabs a slice of pizza and fries. She chats animatedly to the guy in front of her in line and says something in Spanish to the janitor when she sees him carrying big black trash bags toward a side door. Whatever she said makes him laugh.

I examine a plastic container of pasta salad and decide to take it, before grabbing an apple and a bottle of water. Then I follow Mila through the noisy cafeteria to a table along the north wall, where I see Kaleb sitting with two other guys. Mila drops her tray down and hip-checks the East Asian guy's shoulder. "Shove over, Ant. We have a guest."

The guy moves over, glaring up at Mila, and says, "I have nothing but hate and negative regard for you, you know that, right?" But when he glances up at me, he grins, showing off shiny silver braces. "Hey, New Girl," he says, and his voice sounds like the farthest keys on the low side of the piano—rich and heavy. "I'm Anton. You can call me whatever you want, except Ant. I hate when people call me Ant." He gives Mila the finger, and then sticks it in her ear. She shrieks and slaps at his arm, almost knocking a camera off the table.

"Watch those elbows, woman," Anton says, clutching the camera to his chest. "You almost made Frida fall."

"Frida is the camera?" I ask.

"Oh yes, you'll get to know her well," Anton promises.

"Private School, this is everyone. Everyone, Private School. Or, you know, Jordyn," Mila says.

The white guy sitting on the other side of Kaleb has shaggy blond hair and glasses. He's in shorts and a turquoise polo that makes his basil-green eyes pop. "Hey," he says. "Bryce. The glue that holds these goobers together." Mila rolls her eyes and Anton shakes his head, and if Bryce sees, he pretends not to. He stands up and leans across the table to shake my hand, and his grin is broad and bright. I put my tray down so I can reach back.

Bryce clears his throat. "Kaleb says you handed Roderick his ass. That's so hardcore," he says. "Wish I could have been there. He's such a dick." He blushes a little, like he doesn't say words like *dick* very often.

I grin, say it was my pleasure, and take a bow, which makes them all laugh.

"Ugh, stop being so cute," Mila says, throwing a fry at my head.

I catch it; dip it in Anton's ketchup, making sure to give Frida a wide berth; and eat it. "Can't help it. It's in my blood," I reply. Mila is delighted by this exchange, though she tries hard to hide it. But I see her dimple.

"I saw her first," Kaleb tells his friends. He grabs my arm and tugs me down to sit beside him, and I pop open my pasta salad feeling like these are definitely my kind of people.

"So, we obviously need to hear the firsthand account of how the Roderick battle royale went down," says Mila. She points at me with one of her fries.

I look at Kaleb. "You start," I tell him, and he does.

We spend the majority of the lunch period telling and retelling the story—giving different details to Mila, who wants to know how the other people in the class were reacting, and showing Anton Roderick's facial expressions so he can mimic them. Bryce wants to hear Kaleb's closing one-liner over and over, and he laughs in a series of goofy hiccups every time. By the end of lunch, it doesn't feel like I just met these people; it feels like we've known one another awhile. I don't know what to do with good feelings like that, so I just hide my smiles.

"And so we have detention for *two weeks*. Starting this afternoon," Kaleb announces.

Everyone boos.

Mila says, "That's such BS. We should do something about it. Roderick's so problematic. He shouldn't just get away with being awful."

I don't say what I'm thinking—that no one would listen, that it would be our word against his. But Mila looks like she has an idea. "Leave it to me," she says.

"So," Anton pipes up when almost everyone's food is gone. It still surprises me how much his voice is like a late-night radio DJ's, the sound exiting his throat in a miniature thunderstorm. "The expulsion." He smirks and lifts one eyebrow. "Inquiring minds want to know." The grip on my plastic fork tightens, and my face burns. I'm a bit taken aback that my mood can change so drastically so quickly. But this question is exactly what I'd been afraid of.

"OMG, Anton," Mila says. "You can't just ask someone why they got expelled." She shoves his shoulder and he rocks backward, pinwheels his arms like he's about to fall off the bench. Bryce pretends to catch him and pats him on the shoulder like he just saved his life. But soon, one by one, their eyes come back to rest on me. I keep my face smooth, shrug, and poke at the last few pieces of pasta on my tray.

"No, it's okay. I figured it would come up—"

"Oh thank God," Mila says, cutting me off. "I'm sorry, I've been dying to know but, like, trying to respect your privacy or whatever."

Kaleb laughs and shakes his head, and Bryce smiles, but he's quietly watching me too, in a way that makes it clear he also wants to know but his manners mean he'd never have asked. Anton pretends to hold out a mic in my direction. "The floor's yours."

"You all listened to the podcast?" I ask as a way of delaying the inevitable.

"Well, you know I did," Mila answers first, then points to Anton. "He swears he hates it, but he is definitely a devoted listener."

"I catch it every now and then," Bryce says next.

"And I never listen to it, but I don't need to with this one around," Kaleb adds, pointing at Mila. "She gives me the play-by-play every week, like she's an announcer at a game. I don't know why I just used a sports analogy. I'm not a sports gay, I swear."

I smile a little, nod. "So, I got expelled because of a lie someone told on me. I don't really want to get into it, but what she said happened didn't happen. Unfortunately she was the daughter of the dean of students, and I was just me, so." There's more I could say, about how we ended up where we ended up, about what really happened. But this half-truth is all I can bear to tell them. For now. "The last few months were pretty dark because she turned all my friends against me. My parents were beyond disappointed, my friends stopped speaking to me, and I didn't know what was going to happen—if any other school would give me another chance. Let's just say it was not a good summer. The only thing that helped was this." I pull out my sketchbook. "Well, that and therapy."

"Wow. That sucks," Bryce says.

"Yeah," Kaleb agrees.

"Ugh. Was she?" Mila asks with a raised eyebrow, and me and Anton laugh.

The weight of the conversation falls away and I nod again.

"She was," I say, giggling.

"She was what?" Bryce asks.

"White, Bryce. She was white," Kaleb says, casual as anything. He downs the rest of his soda as me, Mila, and Anton laugh louder. The tips of Bryce's ears turn pink.

# 3

Detention is, unsurprisingly, located in the Attic. I make my way up to the small, windowless room at the end of the day without texting my mom. I don't want to lie, but I can't tell her I got detention on my second day of school without context. And it would be impossible to give her all the context she'll need to understand Roderick over text.

There are a few other kids already there when I walk in: a South Asian kid with double-pierced ears in a long green dress, a Black guy wearing Jordans and cutoffs, and Kaleb. He glances up and grins at me when I walk in, so I head in his direction. But when I go to set my bag down at the desk next to him, already whispering about something Mila told me in last period, the teacher chaperoning us—Ms. Lochlin—tells me to find another seat.

"No sitting with friends, Miss..." She jiggles her mouse to wake up her computer and glances at the screen. "Jones, yes?" I nod. "Right. This is not a place for socializing." When she points vaguely to the other side of the room, Kaleb rolls his eyes, and I sigh, but I relocate to sit in a row alone, diagonally behind the guy wearing the Jordans. I take out my phone to text Kaleb, and when I send him a video that makes him laugh out loud, Ms. Lochlin looks up, clears her throat, and points to the whiteboard behind her, on which detention rules are scrawled in blue marker.

*No talking.*

*No phones.*

*No laptops or tablets.*

*No food or drink, except water.*

*No sleeping.*

*No leaving until the hour is complete—use the restroom beforehand and come prepared.*

*Be on time. More than one tardy without documentation will result in additional or weekend sessions.*

*Skipping sessions without documentation will result in in-school or out-of-school suspension.*

I groan and tuck my phone back into my bag, looking over at Kaleb so we can roll our eyes together. Then I pull out the book we were assigned today in English. I'm about to start reading, until I glance at the boy seated in front of me. He has his head down low, his fresh fade showing off an intricately cut shape-up, and it looks like he's drawing. I can tell by the way his pencil flits across the page in front of him—the way his hands move when he puts the pencil down; like he's smearing thin lines into something wider, wilder, like a shadow, a sweep of hair, the curve of a jawline. I lean forward to try and see beyond his forearms, which he has braced around his desk like a protective fence. I lean forward so far, in fact, that my own pencil rolls off the edge of my desk and into the side of the boy's shoe.

He glances down at the pencil, then back and up at me. Sees me leaning over, looking at him. He smirks and I freeze. He's much prettier than I expected him to be—all long eyelashes and thick, full lips. His skin is the color of steeped English Breakfast tea before I add any milk, his eyes and hair a few shades darker. I immediately want to draw him.

"Hey," he whispers. I feel my whole face heat imagining how I must look to him, leaning forward as far as I am with my head cocked at an odd angle. I lean away slowly until my butt is firmly back in my seat.

"Um." I look down, feeling my cheeks heat. "Hi," I whisper back.

"You drop this?" he asks, reaching down and grabbing the pencil. It's hot pink and says DRAW YOUR HEART OUT along the side.

"Oh yeah, thanks. Not to be weird, but can I see what you're working on?"

He laughs, chews on his bottom lip for a second, and looks down at his desk. "Well, that is pretty weird of you—sorry, I didn't catch your name."

"I'm Jordyn," I say, feeling relieved he doesn't already know.

"Jordyn. Cool. I'm Izaiah," says the beautiful boy, touching a hand to his own chest. "And this one isn't quite ready for other people's eyes yet."

I nod. "I totally get that." I hesitate for a second before adding, "I draw too."

"Oh, word?" he whispers back. I'm about to pull out my sketchbook to show him when a brash voice butts into our conversation.

"Mister Thompson, Miss Jones, need I remind you about our silence policy here in detention? You should be using this time to complete homework or other assignments, not to socialize," Ms. Lochlin says before she lowers her glasses and raises her eyebrows.

"Sorry," we both mutter, but when I look back over at Izaiah, he's still grinning at me.

———

Instead of reading for English, I put away my book and spend the rest of the hour sketching a shadowy outline of Izaiah's profile, his wide nose and pouty mouth. The curve of his forehead gives me a little trouble, only because at the place where it meets his hairline, he has a sharp, angled shape-up. I'm better at curves and swoops, soft and blurred edges, than hard, straight lines. I erase and start again, erase and start again before moving on to his temple and ear and the nape of his neck. Instead of finishing it off with the kinda boring curve of his head, I fill the space with random doodles and words, homey little rooms and wispy clouds. I pretend I can read him and these are all the things that fill his thoughts. I fold the sketchbook closed and tuck my pencil into the side pocket of my backpack before pulling out my book again, but I've spent so much time drawing Izaiah, inhabiting the world of what I imagine his mind might be like, that as soon as I turn the first page, Ms. Lochlin says we're free to go.

"So," Izaiah says when we can finally talk without Ms. Lochlin's interruptions. "What are you in for?"

"Ah," I say, grinning. "Disorderly conduct. Yelled at a teacher because he was arguing with me about digital Blackface not being real."

Izaiah whistles. "Whew," he mutters. "That's a good one."

I laugh. "And you?"

"Talked back to the teacher after being asked to put my phone away three times, but I'd just gotten an email from a scholarship I'd been waiting to hear back about."

"Guessing you got it?"

"I did! So when I saw the email come in, I had to read it. Then I had to text my moms and tell her. Then I just wanted to look at the email again—kinda couldn't believe it was real, you know? Three strikes, ya boy was out."

I grin.

Kaleb comes over, says hi, and asks if I had a good detention. "Spent it drawing, so it was cool," I say, tapping the cover of my sketch-book. I could be imagining things, but I think Izaiah looks at it like he's curious.

"God, I was so bored," Kaleb says. "Remind me to bring something interesting to read tomorrow. All I had was this." He holds up the same book from English I was going to start. Both me and Izaiah laugh. When Kaleb asks if I'll walk out with him, I say I'll meet him at his locker after I run to the bathroom. He blows me a kiss as he exits the room and I pretend to catch it. I stand up and Izaiah does too. He towers over me, and while I usually hate being short, I like the particular way his height makes me feel small.

"Maybe I'll see you around, Izaiah," I say, smiling at him as I slip my books and sketchbook into my bag.

"Hope so," he says. "And I, uh, shoulda told you before. My friends call me Zay."

———

The whole way home I keep thinking about Zay. How his name sounds like the first note of a song, or like it could mean rain in another language. I text Kaleb, *What do you know about Zay Thompson?* And he texts back, *Only that I'd like to do bad things to him.*

I laugh out loud on the city bus I'm riding home, and three of the other passengers frown at me. We're stuck in rush hour traffic, and people on the 5:10 p.m. bus are crankier than they are on the 3:50 one I usually take. I mouth a *Sorry* to my fellow riders and then text Mila and ask her the same question.

*Oh, he's a star soccer player, the only reason our crappy athletics department is on anyone's radar. He's really nice and smart too—I had Algebra 2 with him last year. Why?*

I should not be thinking about a boy when I have so many other things going on, but I want to know him, want to learn more about what really goes on in his mind. I take out my sketchbook and a pencil, adding a soccer ball to the crowd of doodles floating in the space above Zay's head.

Mila texts again a few minutes later. *You into him?*

*No clue. I just met him. But he's cute.*

*Uh, yeah*, Mila sends back, and I grin. But *I've heard things about him and girls. He's kind of a player.*

*Oh*, I send, feeling disappointed.

*I wouldn't let that stop me though.*

I laugh again. Of course that wouldn't stop Mila. I'm starting to see that once that girl sets her sights on something or someone, she's gonna get what she wants. I want to be more like her— determined and devoted, and brave like Kaleb too. Funny like Anton, and polite and quietly confident, like Bryce. It's strange but comforting to have met so many people in such a short time who make me want to be different; who make me want to be better. I hope they're as good as I think they are, as good as they make me feel. Because I know from experience that sometimes, when people seem too good to be true, they are.

---

"So, you up there acting a fool already, huh?"

Mom meets me at the door as I walk in, late. Apparently at Edgewood, when a student gets detention, the parents get a phone call. Mom's probably been waiting for me since our normal teatime (a little after four), and it's nearly six o'clock.

"I just don't believe it," another voice says. It's sweet and slow, and I know instantly my auntie Romy must be lounging in my living room too. "They gotta be lying on my baby."

I walk deeper into the house and dive into my auntie's arms. She comes over at least once a week, and I'm always happy to see her because she's the one person who has always made me feel like it's okay to be me—even at my worst. She looks so much like my mom that from behind, I can get them confused if they're facing away from me, but Romy has thicker eyebrows, rounder cheeks, and raised moles across her cheekbones. She calls them "enthusiastic freckles." I'm twirling one of Romy's curls around my finger, ready to catch her up on everything, when I spot my dad in his recliner. I sit up but scoot closer to her, like maybe she'll protect me from the disappointed look he's giving me. Auntie Romy rubs my arm.

"What were you thinking, talking back to a teacher? After everything we went through at Hartwell, you get to Edgewood and do this on your second day?"

I say, "But, Daddy—"

My mom cuts me off. "There's just no excuse for this kind of behavior, Jordyn."

"I'm not trying to make excuses," I say, standing up. "I'm trying to explain."

"Maybe you should hear her out, Joelle," Auntie Romy says to my mom, but my parents are clearly too angry to listen.

"I'll hear her out tomorrow," my mother says. "We shouldn't talk now when emotions are running so high. Either way, I don't want to hear your TV on in that room tonight."

My dad nods in agreement, and he's still frowning as he says, "Homework and bed, that's all you're doing for the foreseeable future."

I give my aunt one more withering look, and she gives me one of encouragement back. She mouths, *It'll be all right, baby girl,* and even though the entire interaction reminds me too much of everything that happened when I was in trouble at my old school—how my parents didn't believe me, the way I was punished before what really happened became clear—for some reason I believe her.

In my room, I studiously complete my homework, and when I finish, it's easy to ignore the TV. I put on my headphones, pull out my sketchbook, and start drawing. I sketch cups of tea left on a table to get cold, my auntie's round face and dozens of moles, my dirty socks in the corner. I hum along to the music and imagine what my life will be like when I no longer have to answer to teachers like Roderick, or even my parents. When I'm eighteen, and a star student at a prestigious art school, and everything about Hartwell and Edgewood is behind me.

Truth is, it's hard for me to linger on my mother's upset or my father's disappointment, because all in all, I had a pretty great day. Kaleb was kind to me, and all his friends (feels too soon to call them my friends) are so, so great. Not to mention a beautiful boy with an even more beautiful name smiled at me. I drew and read and felt less alone than I have in months. So I write my parents a letter. I tell them I'm sorry, that I'll try to be better, that they're right about Edgewood being my chance at a fresh start. Then I explain what happened with Roderick, how I felt helpless until Kaleb spoke up. How standing up beside him made me feel powerful, made me feel like I'm a good person. A better one than I have been. I slip the letter under their bedroom door.

Auntie Romy pokes her head into my room to say goodbye just before she's planning to leave, and I end up telling her everything too because I know that she'll listen and I know she'll believe me. The same way she was the only one who did when everything went down at Hartwell.

Elise Murphy tossed her blond hair over her shoulder and reapplied her lip gloss, leaning over the sink to get as close as she could to the mirror. She liked to go the tiniest bit beyond her lips to make them look a little bigger. Yasmine Thorne had hair that was long and wavy and red, and she flipped the long ribbon of it forward and backward a few times, then picked at the roots with her fingertips, though I couldn't see a difference in the before and after. She painted some reddish-brown liquid eyeliner along her lash line, which made her forest-green eyes take on the shade of moss. Lilliana Sandoval's hair was thick and black, the only thing about her (other than her name and the fragrant lunches she sometimes brought to school) that betrayed her father's Peruvian roots. She also had light brown skin, but most people dismissed it as a tan. Lilly straightened her hair clips, taking them out and putting them back in so that the errant strands around her temples were pulled smooth and secured just above her ears. Then she pulled some foundation out of her bag and patted a bit under her eyes.

As my friends fixed their hair and makeup, I just stood there. I didn't really wear makeup and had flat ironed my hair that morning. If I wanted it to stay as straight as it was, I knew I needed to touch it as little as possible. Sometimes I wished I could wear my hair in braids or puffs, but those styles were against Hartwell's dress code. It was probably for the best. I knew my natural hair would make me stick out here even more than I already did.

"Oh my God," Elise said. "Did you see what Sara had on this morning?"

"Her uniform?" I asked. I washed my hands just for something to do, even though I hadn't peed.

Yasmine looked at me and rolled her eyes, while Lilly giggled. "You're hilarious, Jordyn," she said.

I shrugged.

Elise's lip gloss was a shade of bright pink I could never wear because it would look garish; clown-like against my cinnamon-brown skin. But I thought it looked great on Elise—feminine, natural, and shiny. I absently studied myself in the mirror and smoothed my still-wet thumb and forefinger over my eyebrows, taming the wild, dark hairs.

"No," Elise said, glancing down the length of sinks at me. "Not her uniform, smartass. She had on the most *hideous* shoes I've ever seen."

I thought back, trying to remember if I'd even noticed Sara's shoes that morning. I couldn't place them, but it was snowy out, January having taken a sharp turn toward the cold after winter break this year instead of before it, so I wondered if Sara had been wearing boots. I laughed. "Were they boots? I don't know about Sara's, but there has been some pretty hideous winter footwear this season. And people don't even bother cleaning off the salt stains." I stuck out my tongue like I was disgusted, and when Elise giggled, I felt something like relief course through me.

"And what about," Elise continued, "Landon Miller's breath?" She pretended to gag. "He asked to borrow my pencil in second period and I thought I was going to need a gas mask. I swear I'd die if he was ever my lab partner."

Yasmine and Lilly cracked up, while I only smiled. Landon was nice, so it felt weird to hear Elise giving him such a hard time. But I played along. I always played along. "Oh my God, E! Did you actually say that to him?" I asked Elise.

"No, but I definitely cringed when he asked me. I swear I couldn't help it!" She laughed, and Yasmine and Lilly kept laughing. So did I.

"You're so dramatic," I said, because I wasn't sure what else to say. I knew I couldn't tell Elise what I really thought without turning the meanness in my direction. It had happened before. I didn't want it to happen again.

"What can I tell ya? I was born to perform," Elise said with a wink.

As I dried my hands, I listened as my friends talked about other things until the bathroom door swung open. Aubrey Day walked in with her head down, one earbud hanging out of her ear. Her pale skin was covered in pink bumps and angry red scars. Some of the blemishes were weeping, while others erupted with white, like tiny snowcapped mountains, and her glasses were thick and smudged. Her uniform shirt was a little wrinkled. I smiled at her and wished I could tell her to leave, to turn around and go back the way she came, at least until they were done in there. But I stayed quiet, and Aubrey didn't smile back. As soon as Elise saw her, she started in, the way she always did.

"Look who it is! The great Aubrey Day has decided to grace us with her presence!"

Aubrey kept her head down and ducked into the stall closest to the door so she didn't have to walk past any of us. I had tried to hide Aubrey's paper when Mr. Tucker had me pass back quizzes that morning, but Elise still saw. Aubrey got a 98. Elise got an 80. And as soon as I saw the eighteen-point difference, I knew this or something like it would happen next.

"You think you're soooo smart, don't you?" Elise said. Most people didn't know how hard Elise worked for the grades she got. She had a tutor and spent most weekends studying. Elise's father was the dean of students, and he regularly popped into her classes to "say hello." Everyone knew Mr. Murphy was doing it to make sure Elise was behaving—to make sure she was doing exactly what he wanted her to be doing and nothing else. It clearly messed with her, but whenever I tried to ask her about it, she brushed me off, said he just wanted what was best for her, and changed the subject. I couldn't help but think of that conversation again as I watched Elise stalk over to Aubrey's stall and kick the door. "You think you're smarter than all of us, don't you?"

"At least I got here on my own."

The smallest voice came from behind the door, Aubrey's feeble attempt to stand up for herself. I covered my face with my hands. If Aubrey knew what was good for her, she'd stay quiet like I'd told her to. But then she spoke again. "At least my daddy isn't the only reason I'm not failing."

Elise coughed out a loud, fake laugh. She turned to face us, and I expected her to look pissed. But there was something else, something sad, behind the rage in her brown eyes. And it was like a chain reaction, the way Yasmine and Lilly came to her rescue. Yasmine picked up her water bottle from the edge of the sink and stepped into the stall next to Aubrey's. She climbed onto the toilet, unscrewed the lid of her bottle, and dumped the contents over Aubrey's head without an ounce of hesitation. Aubrey screamed.

"Oh my God," Elise said, but she was laughing, thrilled at this turn of events—that her friends could be cruel too. "You're so crazy!"

Not to be outdone, Lilly grabbed her loose powder foundation, and when Aubrey opened the door of her stall to attempt an escape, Lilly tossed more than half the container in her direction. The tawny powder caked Aubrey's thin hair, face, and white collared top instantly, sticking thanks to the water, making her look like she'd just been unearthed, dug up like a fossil; probably ruining her uniform for good. Elise smiled maliciously, and I just stood there, mouth wide with shock, the pit of my stomach aching.

"At least my father can afford this school," Elise spat into the silence. "At least"—she laughed, and narrowed her eyes—"I *have* a father."

My throat went tight. Elise only knew that Aubrey's dad was MIA because I had told her.

"Harsh, Elise," Lilly said, like *that* was where the whole encounter went off the rails.

I couldn't bring myself to speak.

"We should go," Yasmine suggested. "Before she starts crying or something."

I swallowed hard but followed my friends as they grabbed their bags and filed out of the restroom. I didn't look back at Aubrey as we left.

# 4

"Free Kaleb and Jordyn! Sign the petition to free Kaleb and Jordyn from the clutches of detention!"

I hear Anton yelling down the length of the senior hall when I walk into school the next day. I recognize his rumbling, bass-filled voice immediately. Mila is right behind him, and she's collecting signatures too, but taking a much more subtle approach. By the time I reach them, I'm losing the fight against the overwhelming urge I have to reach out and cover Anton's mouth with my open hand.

Absolutely everyone is staring.

"Oh my God, Anton," Mila says, rolling her eyes. "You could literally just walk up to people and explain the situation. Ain't no reason to be all loud. Hey, Private School," she adds when she looks up and sees me. Today her hair is in two long braids and she's wearing a bunch of silver necklaces. Purple-painted toenails peek out from the hem of her maxi dress in strappy sandals. "Told you to leave it to me." She grins wide, dimples on full display, and winks.

"What are you guys doing?" I whisper-shout. "And, Anton, for the love of God, stop screaming."

"We're gonna spring you, New Girl," Anton says. "No friend of ours is gonna be stuck serving an unjust detention sentence."

I smile, because he called me their friend, but I shake my head too. "I appreciate the gesture, I do, but we tried to explain the situation to the vice principal yesterday when we were first sent to the office. And I tried to tell my parents last night. No luck in either case. What makes you think this will be any better?"

"There's power in numbers, my friend," says Anton. He bops the top of my head with his clipboard, and I duck out of the way, patting my 'fro to make sure he didn't flatten the top. "I mass texted it too," Anton continues, reaching into the pocket of his ripped jeans to pull out his phone. He shows me the message, thick brows furrowed in concentration as he taps through to show where the petition link leads. "Digital signatures will seriously up the ante."

"Did you tell her it was my idea? The texting part, I mean." I turn to see Bryce walking over to us, his hands in the pockets of his chinos. His boat shoes are untied, like always—so much messier than the rest of him. He does that boy band hair flip thing, to get his long bangs out of his eyes. Then he wiggles his eyebrows.

"Brilliant, right?" Bryce asks. Kaleb walks up too and comes over to stand by me. He settles his chin on Mila's shoulder.

"It is absolutely increasing our reach," Mila agrees without conceding that Bryce is brilliant, which I think Bryce notices. Kaleb sighs and whispers, "My heroes." I look around at all of them, feeling my heart swell.

"Thank you, guys. I . . . I can't believe you'd do all this for me."

"Injustice anywhere is a threat to justice everywhere," Bryce recites, a finger lifted in the air like he's giving a speech "And like I said, Roderick's the worst."

"I mean, I'm mostly doing it for Kaleb," Anton mutters, but he gives me a quick grin. "Kidding!" he sings, and I laugh to keep myself from happy crying because I can feel my loneliness disappearing the longer I stand surrounded by them. I can feel something growing between us that could become real trust, real friendship. Mila socks Anton in the arm anyway. He falls back into the lockers, hand over his huge and heaving heart.

First period is fairly uneventful, all things considered. Roderick gives Kaleb and me quick, loaded looks but otherwise behaves himself. There are no inappropriate jokes—no awkward, uncomfortable moments due to his casual slights. Instead he sticks to the software we're talking about today, doesn't attempt to be funny, delivers his lecture and our assignments with barely any personality or flair. It's impressively boring, and I find myself fighting sleep. I doodle a quick sketch of Kaleb in the margins of my notes to stay awake, focusing on his expertly arched eyebrows, which are thick, dark, and even, and the graceful way his curls frame his face.

"Maybe the messiness was his whole personality," I say to Kaleb after class. "Because that was brutal."

"God, can you imagine being that uninteresting? So lacking in creativity that making fun of people and subtle racism are your only ways of making friends?"

"And think about the *kinds* of friends you'd make if that's all you have going for you."

Both Kaleb and I shudder.

"At least we don't have that problem," Kaleb says, shimmying, taking my hand, and twirling me around. The skirt I'm wearing flares, blooming like a flower. "Is it a burden for you the way it is for me? Being so flawless?"

I giggle. "Is it ever," I say. "Utterly exhausting."

---

All day people come up to me asking what the petition is about, the details of what Roderick did, if talking back to teachers is why I was expelled from my old school. I dodge most of what they ask by answering their questions with a question in return: Did they speak to Anton or Mila? What have they heard? Have they ever seen anyone get expelled for something like that?

By lunch Mila reports that they already have fifty signatures, and by the end of the day Anton tells me they have over a hundred.

"How many kids go to this school?" I ask Kaleb as we walk to detention together.

"Ummm, maybe like a couple thousand."

"Wow," I mutter. Hartwell has five hundred students, total. "How many signatures do you think they'll get?"

"Who knows," Kaleb answers. "But I'm sure they'll get a lot. Everyone knows how Roderick is. But most people just ignore him. I'm glad we didn't. Bystanders are the worst."

I feel a guilty tug deep in my chest, but I nod in agreement.

I try not to look at Zay as I walk into detention because I don't want Ms. Lochlin to tell me I can't sit near him the way she did with me and Kaleb. So I keep my eyes and hands busy with my phone, walking to the seat beside him, pretending to text before I tuck it away in my bag for the next hour.

Zay's drawing again. When I finally let myself look over at him, I can tell by the way his back is hunched over his desk, by the way he's hiding his work. I don't know if it's the same thing he was working on yesterday or if it's something new, but I take out my sketchbook too. I rip off a corner of a page and write *How long have you been drawing? I started when I was six.* I wait until Ms. Lochlin looks back down at the romance novel she's reading, and then I tap his elbow. Zay turns and smiles like he's surprised to see me there. I guess he was so focused on his drawing he didn't notice me come in.

"Hey you," he whispers. I put my finger over my lips and nod at the note. Then I look back at my own sketchbook, opening it to a fresh, blank page. I decide to sketch Ms. Lochlin. Her long braids alone will be a challenge, and I need something to help pass the time. I glance over at Kaleb. He's reading a thick paperback, one of the fantasy novels from the series he told me he's obsessed with, and it makes me want to draw Lochlin as a dragon. I'm still working on the first pointy, scaly wing, making it spring out from behind her desk chair, draped and heavy like a stage curtain, when Zay places the note back on my desk.

*Started when I was ten. Even wanted to go to an art school. But my pops really wanted me to play soccer. My gogo is South African and she was pressin me too.*

*Gogo?* I write back.

I see his shoulders shake as he laughs. *Yeah. My grandmother.*

We're going to need a new piece of paper soon, covered as the tiny slip is already, front and back. But I squeeze in one last thing before I plan to rip out a new sheet: *I wanted to go to an arts high school too, but my parents wanted me to have a more "well-rounded" education. Their words, not mine. Now I just know that'll be my plan for college.*

Zay nods when he reads my most recent note. Then he crumples it into a tiny ball, tosses it into his open bag, and wisely rips a full page out of his sketchbook.

*I had this whole thing about only applying to art schools for college too, then I got this soccer scholarship, so it's pretty much been decided for me. But I think I like it better this way.*

*What do you mean?* I write back.

*Now when I draw, if I draw, it's just for me.*

I smile and nod. It makes sense.

*What do you like to draw?* I ask him next.

*People mostly. Animals. Cars too.*

I read his answer, then add: *I like portraits, and I usually give them a bit of an unrealistic twist, but I'm not anti–still life or landscape. A pile of dirty dishes with food floating above it, a stack of books with the characters coming to life. But yeah, mostly people for me too. People as I see them anyway.*

Zay writes: *You ever worry people will think you're creepy if you draw them?*

*Well, I hadn't . . . but now I'll feel like a creep every time. Thanks for that.*

Zay laughs loudly enough that Ms. Lochlin looks up. He starts coughing, trying to pretend that's what was happening all along, and I bite my bottom lip and stare hard at the desk in front of me.

Instead of writing another note, I flip back in my sketchbook to the picture I'd drawn of Zay. I add pencils and charcoal and a sketchbook to the things floating along the top of the page, the things filling his head. Along the bottom of the drawing I write, *Hope this isn't creepy*. As soon as Ms. Lochlin looks away, I rip the page out and slide it onto the edge of Zay's desk. He covers his mouth so he won't laugh out loud again, but then he stares at my picture of him for a really long time.

At the end of detention, as we stand to pack our bags, he clears his throat roughly and says, "You're really good." He tries to give me the drawing and I shake my head, pushing it back toward him.

"It's yours," I say. "And thanks. I still want to see some of your stuff. No rush, of course, just whenever you're ready."

Zay nods, and then he slowly opens his sketchbook to one of the earliest pages, near the very front. He nibbles on his lower lip like he's nervous, then he turns the sketchbook, so it's facing me. On the page is a really detailed drawing of a small bird perched on the top of a park bench. His work is more realistic than my stuff, more solidly rooted in true-to-life details. The pencil lines are thin and straight, unbroken and solid in a way mine rarely are. I can see each individual feather in the bird's wings, the splintering wood of the bench.

"Wow," I say. "So are you."

He rubs the back of his neck. "I'm aight," he mutters. "If you want to see some of my other stuff, you can follow me. I post a lot of my work when it's finished. You can . . . tell me what you think." He ducks his head like he's embarrassed. Which is adorable.

I ask for his handle. Search it and hit follow. Then I put my phone back in my pocket even though I want to scroll through his entire feed right now.

"Follow me back, maybe," I say before I turn to go.

"Will do, Tiny."

And just like that, I have yet another nickname. My chest fills with warmth.

---

"I read your letter," Mom says as soon as I get home from school. She's waiting in the kitchen like normal, even though it's late, and she has the kettle on. "And Romy yelled at me."

Daddy walks into the room a second later too and sits down. He has a small take-out box in his hand with the Bread & Butter logo on it—a stylized *B&B*—that he puts in the center of the table. He licks his lips and says, "Honey, come sit with us."

I look from them to my room and back to the two of them again.

"Um . . . Is this a trap?" I ask.

My mom shakes her head and my dad kinda laughs.

"No, sweetie, no. We're sorry. Sit down." She hands me a cup of tea.

"Romy called me this morning. Told me what you told her. Told me that if I didn't go down to that school to speak to someone about that teacher's behavior, she would. She told me that I should have listened to you. When I finally got her off the phone, I read your letter, then told your father about it. I hate to admit it, but my big sister is almost always right."

I look down, into my cup. "Yeah. It kinda sucked that you wouldn't hear me out."

I shouldn't have been surprised. After everything that happened last year, my parents' reaction let me know, again and again, that I let them down, so I should have known any misstep would lead to me feeling like I am a disappointment to them. My chest feels cold and empty when I think about it for too long, the way I'm not sure if my parents truly believe I'm a good person. So I tell them about the only thing making me feel better lately, like I might not be as awful as they (or I) believe. I tell them about Mila and Kaleb and Bryce and Anton.

"A few friends are collecting signatures. They're going to petition the vice principal to let us out of detention early. I don't think it will work—the VP seems like she's very much on the side of any and all teachers despite the circumstances—but it's the thought that counts."

Mom nods. Today her locs are twisted up in a tight, high bun and she's wearing all black. She looks sophisticated and stylish—not at all like a mom.

"Romy yelled, huh?" I ask, starting to smile.

"She did. It was scary." I laugh and my mom shakes her head. "Do you want me to go to the school? Or do you want to handle this yourself? It sounds like you were in the right and you have the support of your friends, but I'm happy to come back you up." I'm surprised she offered, but I don't let on.

I sip my tea and shake my head, thinking about Anton's booming voice and Mila getting the lunch ladies and the janitorial staff to sign her clipboard too.

"I think we got it. And anyway, I don't mind detention so much."

She looks more closely at me, and though I don't say anything about Zay, I think her mom-intuition is telling her that there must be a boy. She grins a little.

Daddy doesn't say anything, just opens the take-out box. It's heavy with two thick slices of pound cake so buttery the outside of the box is dark in a few places with oil stains. He lifts a piece and settles it onto a saucer. Slides it my way without a word. My father communicates with food: hearty meat dishes when he wants to talk; soups and stews when he wants to offer comfort; all your favorites heaped together when he's proud of you. Desserts are how he apologizes.

"Okay. If you say so," Mom says as I tuck the first bite of cake into my mouth. It's moist and sweet and rich, like guilt, like pleasure. I close my eyes. "And I'm so sorry I didn't listen to you, sweetie. Your father is too."

Daddy nods before standing to open the freezer. He pulls out vanilla ice cream, serves me a scoop, and kisses my forehead. "My bad, honey," he whispers. "My bad."

---

My friends spend the next couple days collecting signatures before and after school and in between classes. I feel so lucky to have found quality people like them so quickly after starting at Edgewood, but a small part of me still doesn't trust it. I wonder how they could benefit from helping me this way—if there could be some ulterior motive. But no matter how I look at it, or who I ask, their intentions seem to be completely pure. It makes something deep inside me vibrate with worry—I don't want them to realize I'm not worth their kindness. And worse: I'm desperate to be worthy.

By Thursday morning, they have collected over seven hundred signatures. And like Bryce thought, the ability to sign it digitally definitely helped—more than half the students signed using the link Anton sent around. Somehow Bryce and Mila land a meeting with the vice principal that neither Kaleb nor I am allowed to be present for, and at lunch on Thursday, they deliver the news that though we have to finish out the remaining days this week, our second week of detention has been canceled.

"What?!" I shout. I'm both impressed and can't really believe it. Kaleb says, "Um ... How did you pull that off?"

"You should have seen Bryce in the meeting," Anton says. "He definitely channeled his politician roots, all serious and somehow still charming. Polite but firm. Big ally energy."

Mila cracks up as Bryce smirks, and I reach over to hug him with one of my arms. Kaleb does the same on his other side, so Bryce is sandwiched between us.

"She also said they'd be observing Roderick's classes over the next couple of weeks to make sure all our concerns are addressed," Bryce tells us.

While I can't believe the administration is taking this so seriously, I roll my eyes. "He'll be on his best behavior if someone is just chillin' at the back of his classroom."

"Yeah," Mila says. She picks at a loose thread on her skirt. "That's exactly what I said."

"I guess it's good they're doing something," Anton says. "They are adults after all, the most incompetent of all age groups."

We all laugh at that.

Bryce clears his throat and looks down at his perpetually untied shoes. "I think I wanna run for president," he says suddenly.

We all stop eating and look at him.

"Of, like, America?" I ask.

Anton covers his mouth, giggling.

"Dang, New Girl," he says. "That's something goofy I would say."

I throw a ketchup packet at him, but he catches it. I poke out my tongue.

"No, no. Of Edgewood," Bryce clarifies. "Student body president."

"Ew. Why?" Mila replies, barely letting him finish his sentence. "I thought you hated all that stuff. You're always talking about how fake your granddad has to be whenever he's campaigning. How performative it all is. How if you wanted to lie, you could do it in your writing."

"Your granddad?" I ask, looking at Bryce.

"Oh yeah, New Girl, guess you don't know. Bryce's grandpa is a senator," Anton says. "His dad has run for office a few times, and Cam, his brother, was in student government too."

"Bryce is the rebel," Mila continues, "but maybe he's tired of just writing his little stories." She knocks her knuckles against a weathered composition notebook that is on the table in front of Bryce. He immediately blushes, grabs it, and shoves it into his backpack.

"I dunno," Bryce says. "Maybe it's this whole thing with Roderick.

Seeing how Vice Principal Harris reacted to us. How she reacts differently to certain students pushing back versus me. Maybe if I were president, students would be able to do more—have more of a voice."

"I mean, I could see it," Kaleb says, jabbing his fork in Bryce's direction. "You're totally the typical president type."

"Good grades," Mila says.

"Teachers love you," Kaleb adds.

"You're tall," Anton says.

I quirk an eyebrow at Anton, and Mila rolls her eyes. Kaleb puts his head down on the table, and Bryce says, "Anton. What?"

"What do you mean what?" Anton says. "That's totally a thing. People always vote for tall people. It's like an evolutionary preference subconsciously stuck in our brains from when we had to fend off predators or something. I swear! Stop looking at me like that. Oh my God. Look it up."

---

I'm more grateful than I expect to be when Friday rolls around. I'm looking forward to a relaxing weekend at home, hanging out with Auntie Romy and watching scary movies, but Mila tells me we'll be busy all weekend, and that I can't leave her with all the "penis-havers." So, all of a sudden, I'm roped into their plans.

On Saturday we protest the loss of reproductive rights in front of the Supreme Court building. It's raining when we step out of the Metro at Union Station, so we buy ponchos from one of the touristy souvenir shops that are printed with the American flag, the Capitol Building, and the Washington Monument. We hold signs above our heads that get soggy in the rain. They read KEEP YOUR ~~PAWS~~ LAWS OFF MY BODY (Mila) and I HAVE A HEARTBEAT TOO (me). Anton's just says THIS IS REALLY BAD. Bryce and Kaleb opted for touristy umbrellas so they could show off their T-shirts that say THIS IS WHAT A FEMINIST LOOKS LIKE. Anton snaps photos with Frida and tells us he'll tag us once he gets home and uploads them. We scream, "My body, my choice," at the top of our lungs and I feel so grateful they brought me with them—that I now have friends who believe in the same things as me. I decide right then and there what I want my zine for Roderick's class to be about, and I turn to Kaleb to see if he wants to work on it with me. "What do you think about making our zine for Digital Design all about student activism?"

His hazel eyes go so wide I can see the whites all around them and he nods more enthusiastically than I expected him to. "Oh, hell yes," he says, and I laugh, grateful we'll have all semester to work on it—both because I know Kaleb will have lots of amazing ideas and because it gives me a legitimate excuse to keep hanging out with all four of them. I can already imagine a spread of interviews with each of them covering the causes they care most about—Mila and animals, Bryce and politics. Anton would probably talk about how art could be activism, using his photography and his work on the school paper as examples. Kaleb seems to care about everything, so I can't wait to interview him too, and I already have ideas about how to lay it all out, organizing the whole thing by topic and finding other students who are as passionate about making a difference in the world as we are.

After, we go to Bryce's house to dry off and brainstorm campaign ideas. It turns out that the notebook Bryce had hurriedly hidden away at lunch the other day is full of scary stories he's written, and when I tell him I'm obsessed with horror too—that I have a collection of Stephen King, that my favorite movies as a kid were the ones that give most children nightmares—I sketch a design for his campaign posters that looks like a still from a zombie movie: students running down Edgewood's hallway being chased by issues from Bryce's platform—zombies with words like *too-short lunch periods*, *student/admin communication*, and *sexist dress code policy* emblazoned in thought bubbles above their heads. After some truly horrendous ideas (mostly from Anton), we come up with a logline for the poster: *High school can feel like a horror movie—only the strong survive. Vote for Bryce, he'll get you out alive.* Bryce lets out one of his loudest, goofiest laughs at that. We come up with a slogan for his campaign too: *Don't roll the dice, vote for Bryce!* We make a plan to create companion versions of the poster where Bryce has slayed all the "issue zombies," him standing triumphantly atop a pile of them.

We also talk strategy, and by the time Bryce's mom orders pizza for us, we have a four-week plan for securing his victory all mapped out, targeting one group of students per week—he'll start with freshman issues, like the broken vending machine in their hallway, and work his way up to senior problems, like funding for the senior prom, right before the vote. "I think my main platform should be about communication though—maybe creating a board of students to bring issues to the administration—kids who can be a voice for the voiceless."

I smile at Bryce when he says this, but Kaleb cuts in, "Maybe pivot that a little? You don't want to speak *for* anyone—because voicelessness isn't real. You want to make sure you're using your influence to elevate voices that are normally silenced. It's a subtle but big difference."

We all get quiet, until Mila snaps her fingers like she's at a poetry slam and says, "Damn, K. Facts."

"Wasn't Cameron class president too?" Kaleb asks, looking up at a family photo over the mantel in Bryce's living room as we pass around slices of pepperoni pizza. In it an older man and woman, clearly Bryce's parents, stand behind their two sons: a younger Bryce and a boy who's a few inches taller, with the same green eyes, though his hair is a darker dirty blond. Bryce's older brother, Cameron, I guess.

Bryce seems to stiffen a little. "Yeah," he says. "He was. Now he's doing poli-sci at Princeton. The folks are just *sooo* proud." He says it sarcastically, with a dark edge coloring his voice. Kaleb looks at Mila out of the corner of his eye and silently takes a bite of his pizza.

We end the night writing victory speeches for him that sound more like the ones comedians deliver at award shows than anything he'd actually say. Anton records Bryce's attempts at reading our goofy speeches, and when he can't get through any of them without laughing, we turn it into a game, each of us taking turns delivering the same one. I'm the only person who can keep a straight face from start to finish, so I win the last slice of pizza. "And bragging rights," Kaleb says. "You have a killer poker face, J. Didn't know you had it in you."

I spend Sunday morning with Mila at an animal shelter where she volunteers, bottle-feeding kittens and taking the dogs on long, slow walks. And all afternoon we try to catch up on schoolwork in her kitchen. I tell her about the zine idea, and even though she's not in the class, she says, "Oooh. Could be an excellent way to low-key call Roderick out with his own assignment." I hadn't thought of that.

"Of course you want revenge," I say to her, laughing.

She smirks. "Only if it's clever and classy."

As we talk and work, her little sisters keep rushing in and out. They're six and two years old and are like mini versions of her with the same wild black hair, the same dimpled grins. They both want to try on my earrings and shoes and are distracting enough that Mila chases them into the basement. When she speaks to them in Spanish, it sounds like music. We give them snacks and turn on *Encanto* so we can work, but they sing off-key so loudly that we give up on homework and watch with them.

When I finally make it home, it's just in time to watch the latest *Halloween* movie with Auntie Romy, who came to hang out with me since my mom's at an art show and Daddy's working late at Bread & Butter. We make bracelets together while we watch Michael Myers being creepy and murderous. Then I look through the photos Anton posted, liking and commenting on them all. He has such an eye for angles and lighting, and I make a mental note to ask him about his editing software because it's clear he's using something subtler than the app's built-in filters. Before bed I sketch the other version of Bryce's campaign poster in my room while listening to a new band Kaleb told me about.

I've almost completely forgotten Tomcat Tea exists when the notification about the newest episode pops up on my phone around midnight, like a bad omen.

Hello, fellow students! We are back again, this time for episode two of the season. It's been an . . . *interesting* first week at Edgewood High. You all have kept me busy this past week, and the school year is only just getting started.

You know what time it is! Here's our weekly recap: In sports, rookie first-year Patrick Smith is looking like he'll break Edgewood's streak of being sucky at basketball. He's only fourteen years old and already six four—Patrick, you might have to fold into a pretzel to fit on the team bus, but you fit perfectly in our hearts. And Izaiah Thompson is continuing to own at soccer, leaving the rest of his teammates to look like amateurs. We're rooting for you, Izaiah and Pat, and everyone else, step it up.

Ahem, excuse me . . . In student government news, the race has begun! Bryce Green has officially put in his bid for class president, following in the footsteps of his older brother. Since we all have Cameron to thank for getting Takis and Twix back into the vending machines, will Bryce be worthy of joining this political dynasty? In not-so-shocking news, his formidable rival, Peyton

Reynolds, has decided to run against him. We all know the competitive history between these two. Is it just me, or does Peyton give golden retriever energy? All pep, no substance—not the best fit for the title of class president. As I said, that's just my opinion. Who do you think will win? Only time will tell, but Bryce has my vote.

Now, what you're all here for is the real tea! Let me tell you, this week's bombshell is *juicy*.

Remember last week, when I said I was suspicious of Scarlett Fisher? Well, new intel just dropped on why she's back at Edgewood after spending sophomore year *elsewhere*, and I had every right to think her return was sus, and you should too. Intuition never lies! I've been hearing that she attended a private school in Maryland last year and was quickly expelled. Sounds like she and Jordyn might have a lot in common! The week's questions are— why did she transfer in the first place, where did she go after being kicked out of school, and of course, why did she get expelled?

You guys know I have my sources, and right now there are two main possibilities: The first is that Scarlett was arrested for attempting to shoplift four thousand dollars' worth of rare tropical fish from a Petco and is actually only returning after a stint in juvie! But on the contrary, I have *also* heard that her rich daddy paid to get her admitted to a prestigious school to better her college chances, only for their money to dry up out of nowhere, leaving her tuition unpaid. It's very possible that there's something shady going down with how her family chooses to use their money, and *that* is why she's back with us "normal people." Time will tell what the real story is.

That's it for this week! Everybody, I'll see you on the next episode of Tomcat Tea. We'll be back with more tea, don't worry. In the meantime, you can send us the latest news throughout the week via Instagram DM, @tomcattea! Stay tuned . . . and stay messy. I *know* you will.

# 5

"Come to my soccer game."

On Tuesday, the last day of our "detention sentence" as Kaleb has taken to calling it, Zay turns to me as soon as Ms. Lochlin tells us we're dismissed. He has a small, crooked smile on his face and he looks a little shy despite the confidence with which he invites me to watch him play, stating it instead of asking. My heart flutters and I smile back.

"When is it?" I ask him, though I know I'll come no matter when or where it is. We've passed sketches of each other back and forth all afternoon, and after I creeped on his account and sent him DMs about every one of his drawings, he sent back blushing emojis and demanded that I stop. He's such a great artist that I need to see him play soccer. Part of me can't believe one person could be that good at two really hard things.

"Tomorrow," he says. "It's a home game against our rival, so we try to pack the field if we can. I mean, not that I'm only inviting you because of that. I'd want you there anyway."

He says all this in a rush, and it's so cute I want to pinch his cheeks. Then he rubs the back of his neck in the way he always does when he feels a little awkward. It's weird to realize I know this about him already. I wonder what he knows about me.

Out of the corner of my eye, I see Kaleb waiting by the door, making kissy-faces. I quickly look away from him, hoping my cheeks don't bloom pink and betray me.

"I don't know jack about soccer. Are there positions other than goalie?"

Zay laughs and seems to relax a bit. "You're hopeless," he says. "But yeah. I'm a striker. Basically means I hang out on the wings and spend most of the game shooting my shot." He looks down at the floor before glancing back up at me through his lashes. "No, uh, pun intended."

This *boy*.

"Ah, so you think you're important, huh?" I tease.

"If you're asking if it's possible for soccer, as a sport, to exist without me, the answer is no."

I let out a surprised snort, because he's usually more reserved than this. I wasn't expecting the quiet confidence behind these jokes, and this whole conversation almost feels like flirting. Zay laughs at the sound I make.

"You mind if I bring friends with me?" I ask him. "Mila Lopez. You know her? Anton Wu might come too."

Mila has been asking for updates on our "budding romance" constantly, so I know she'll appreciate the invitation. And Anton told me he's working on mastering setting shutter speeds manually, and that something with lots of action, like a sport, would be good practice. Plus, I don't want to sit in the stands alone.

"Yeah, Mila's cool. Don't know Anton well, but the more the merrier. So does that mean you'll come?"

"Oh yeah. Did I not say that yet?" I shake my head, trying to get his crooked smile out of my mind so I can think straight. But then he does it again, and this time his eyes crinkle in the corners. I die a little.

"You didn't," he says in a low, amused voice.

"I'll be there," I assure him, glancing up to see Kaleb humping the doorframe. I almost choke. I clear my throat and Kaleb doubles over at the face I must be making. I'm going to kill him. I hook my backpack on my shoulder and head in his direction. But after shooting Kaleb a threatening look, I spin around, walking backward for a few steps so I can say to Zay, "Listen for me yelling your name."

---

"Private School's got a daaaate," Mila sings as soon as we sit down at the lunch table the next day. I waited to tell her about Zay's invitation while we were in the lunch line instead of yesterday specifically so they'd all have less time to tease me about it because I knew they'd come for me. I was right, and now my cheeks heat so quickly that I stare down at my pizza slice, peeling off the pepperonis one by one just so I don't have to make eye contact with anyone.

"Oooh, is it with her detention boo?" Anton asks.

At this point I just completely cover my face with my hands.

Bryce hiccups with laughter, Kaleb screams, and Anton follows up with, "Aw, New Girl, we're happy for you!"

"It's not a date," I mutter, but before I can say anything else, Mila pipes up again.

"He wants her to come to his soccer game, which means she has to wait for him after, *which means* he loves her and he's gonna tell her, basically." Mila shrugs like it's obvious.

"I invited Mila, because it is very much *not* a date. Anton, do you want to come too? I thought you could bring Frida? Maybe get those action shots you were telling me about?"

Anton narrows his already narrowed eyes at me. "Not a bad idea, New Girl."

But Bryce makes a face, like I'm making this all up on the spot. "Sounds *real* legit, Jordyn," he says sarcastically. "I'm sure you're only going so Anton can take photos."

Kaleb snorts and Mila giggles.

"Oh my God, I hate you *all*," I say. But I can't help but laugh too.

"What's going on with the presidential race?" I ask Bryce, desperate to shift the attention to anyone other than me. I don't mention what was said on the podcast about it, but I can tell by Bryce's face that it's heavy on his mind.

He winces and shrugs, pushing his blond bangs out of his eyes. "I started campaigning with the freshmen today like we'd planned, but there's an unforeseen . . . complication."

He pauses dramatically and looks around at us all. "Okay . . . ?" Mila says as we all wait for him to continue.

"Freaking Peyton is running too. She's never said anything about wanting to be involved in student government. But as soon as she heard I was running, she popped up out of nowhere."

"She's probably the only student at Edgewood the teachers love more than Bryce," Mila says in a low voice, right against my ear. "She's smart and popular and has starred in all the school productions since we were freshmen. She's also the only person standing between him and graduating valedictorian like his older brother. Who his parents are *constantly* comparing him to, by the way. He hates her."

"Peyton has everything," Bryce continues, like he didn't hear anything Mila said, and maybe he was so wrapped up in his own thoughts that he didn't. His green eyes seem shadowed behind his smudged glasses. "I'm not gonna let her have this too."

"Dark, Bry," Mila says. "Is this your villain origin story?"

"Every hero has a dark past too," I say, coming to Bryce's defense. "This could be the reason he becomes even more determined to win." I take the opportunity to pull out the poster sketches I made the night before, spreading them across the lunch table.

Everyone oohs and aahs, and Bryce smiles at me. "Good to know someone here is on my side," he says. When he tosses his empty chip bag at Mila's head, crumbs tumbling out and onto her lap, we all laugh.

———

After school I meet Mila and Anton at the edge of the soccer field. Anton lifts Frida and aims the camera at the Edgewood mascot—a six-foot fuzzy orange-and-white tomcat wearing a black-and-blue jersey, currently doing backflips—as he tells us he's going to stay "down here to be closer to the action." Mila and I say we'll find him after, and we make our way onto the densely packed bleachers. All the shady spots are taken, and the soccer moms have set up along the perimeter of the field with their umbrellas and coolers, younger siblings of students on the team playing rough games of tag behind them.

"Why is it still so hot?" Mila says as we settle into our seats in direct sunlight. "It's mid-September." The glint off the metal stands makes it even warmer, and I can feel the sun's heat on my thighs through my jeans. Mila flips her hair forward and twists her long tresses into a messy top bun. Her hairline is already damp with sweat. "I feel for whoever is in that mascot suit," she adds.

"Oof. Me too. But climate change is real," I say, fanning my face. I tie my T-shirt into a knot in the front, just above my belly button, and roll up the bottoms of my jeans. "Also, Zay *is* in our midst."

Mila cracks up, pulls a water bottle from her bag, and takes a long swig. "You have a point, Private School. He's very, *very* hot. So, this crush . . . it's pretty serious, huh?"

I shrug. "Honestly, I haven't had a crush in so long I've kinda forgotten what they feel like."

"No hot guys at Hartwell?" Mila asks, leaning back on her elbows. "I mean, you're cute as hell, so I know people had to be into you."

"It's not that exactly," I say, trying to figure out how much to say. "It's more like I didn't vibe with anyone. Zay's kind and quiet and loves art, like I do. He sees things like I do, you know? So I can talk to him about how the world looks to me and he gets it. It also helps that he's not a rich jerk like most of the guys at Hartwell were."

Mila nods, then grins and waves to someone over my head. I turn to see a Black girl with big box braids and glistening, dark brown skin. "Who's that?" I ask.

"Brit Campbell," Mila says. "My ex. We're cool though."

I'm a little surprised for a second. Not because Mila's ex is a girl, but because it makes me realize I've only known her for a few weeks. Mila, Kaleb, Anton, and Bryce already feel like friends I've had forever, but in this moment I have to admit to myself that it hasn't been very long at all. I don't know much about them. And they hardly know anything about me.

I look at Brit, at the way her hair falls over her shoulders, the way her skin shimmers in the sunlight. I can imagine Mila with her arm around her, how she'd whisper in the other girl's ear, dimples popping, making Brit laugh and blush—the same easy charm Mila showers on everyone. "She's pretty," I say.

"I know," Mila agrees. She points to a few other people at the game: a tall, baby-faced boy in the highest row named Jesus she says she dated as a freshman, a curly-haired blond across the field called Taylor who went out with her for a few months last year, "and Alex," she says. "The one in the ripped jeans leaning against the fence over there? Gave me my first set of tarot cards and taught me how to read them."

I shove her shoulder. "You absolute player!"

"What can I say." Mila shrugs. "I'm easy to love."

"And clearly very humble too," I say, laughing and shaking my head.

A few minutes later, the team runs out onto the field. I stand up and scream Zay's name, but everyone is shouting and clapping, so he doesn't hear me. He looks around, so I jump up and down waving, and I can tell the moment he spots me in the crowd—that shy smile of his creeps over his lips, making his eyes nearly disappear. He waves back before jogging to the center of the field. There's a coin toss, some exchange I can't hear between the coaches, and then Zay is handed the ball. He sets it down, sprints toward it, and kicks it so hard and high that I gasp. The game has started.

And immediately I have no idea what's going on. It just looks like a bunch of running back and forth to me, but I try to pay attention, try my best to keep my eye on the ball. I'm doing pretty well tracking the ball, at least until I hear something too distracting to ignore—a name making its way through the crowd—and it's not Zay's or any other player's from the team.

"I can't believe Scarlett came," someone in front of me says. I follow the angle of her head to see what she does. And there's Scarlett in a black T-shirt and short denim shorts with fishnet stockings, showing off her thick, long legs. Her signature winged eyeliner is heavier and darker than usual, and she's writing or drawing in a notebook at the end of the same row where we're sitting. Her combat boots are untied, the laces loose and dangling.

"I bet Scarlett *did* get arrested," I hear another girl say. She's in a pink tank top and is sitting beside the first one who spoke, right in front of me. "I could totally see her stealing something, or, like, beating someone up. I mean, she's huge."

"But what if she really got her dad to bribe her way into a better school? I took ninth-grade English with her, and she could barely read," says a third girl, this one wearing a tight summer dress, in the same row.

They aren't quiet. I look back, and when Scarlett looks up, I know she can probably hear them. She somehow looks pissed and sad.

"If I am ever on that podcast, I'm staying home for a couple weeks, minimum. Until people forget I exist." They're all nodding and looking in Scarlett's direction.

I look over at Mila, who frowns. She's heard it all too.

"God, do you see her? What's with this look? She wasn't all goth or whatever before. I bet Tomcat Tea is right, and something shady went down."

"Yeah. Girl looks like she's seen some shit."

I feel that ache in my gut that I felt all the time at Hartwell: the same one that made me feel close to being sick in Roderick's class. The feeling that what is happening around me is wrong and I need to say something, do something. The feeling that it's up to me to make something better or to make it right. But I can't move, paralyzed as I am by the fear that they could turn their ire in my direction.

Mila leans forward in her seat before I get up the nerve to. "Lay off her, guys," she says quietly.

All three of the girls sitting in front of us turn.

"Why do you care?" the one in the dress asks.

"I don't need a reason to care about other people," Mila says, an edge to her voice that wasn't there a second ago. "You know the whole point of that podcast is to stir up drama. Why are you letting it?"

I nod in agreement, wishing I had spoken up too but grateful Mila did first. And when one of the other girls in their group rolls her eyes, I feel like it's finally safe for me to speak. My heart is pounding, but knowing Mila agrees they should leave Scarlett alone spurs me forward. "You literally just said if you were on the podcast, you'd stay home for weeks, so you must get it. And even if you don't, take it from me, since I was on there before I even started here—it's trash." I think about Anton asking me about my expulsion, about the way they all looked expectantly at me as I told them as much of the truth as I could bear to reveal. "Why would you want to make school any more hostile for her than it already is?"

They turn away from us then, so I have no idea if what we said to them sank in, but they keep their voices down for the rest of the game. Maybe they do that because they're still talking about Scarlett or maybe they've moved on to talking about me and Mila, but it doesn't matter. I watch Zay score again and again, cheering my head off every time, but in the quieter moments I glance over at Scarlett, wondering if I have a right to defend her. And if I have questions about that, do I deserve friends who defend others without thought the way Mila and Kaleb do? What if I'm not cut out for the responsibility of taking people on—being involved in all these fraught confrontations whenever someone says or does something I don't agree with—if that's what it takes to be a good person? I can't seem to forget the way I used to be: how the old Jordyn would sit here quietly, or worse, even join in with the girls who are criticizing Scarlett. To be worthy of people like Mila and everyone else I've grown so close to so quickly, what if I need to do—and to *be*—more?

———————

When the game ends, Mila says she doesn't want to overstay her welcome and rushes down the bleachers to collect Anton before I can stop her. And as the girls in front of us walk to their cars, they look down their noses at Scarlett, who shoots them dirty looks right back. They immediately scurry away, but something in Scarlett's expression betrays her veneer of toughness. She seems to curl into herself once they're gone, like their words and actions truly hurt her feelings. As Scarlett leaves, Mila and Anton jog over and walk to the parking lot with her, and whatever Mila says makes her smile, while Anton actually makes her laugh. I watch them until Scarlett climbs inside her car and waves goodbye.

When she glances up and sees me looking, I wave and smile, but her expression turns dark before she backs out of the lot without waving back. Her face sends a chill up my spine. I have no idea what this girl has against me. Her animosity almost feels like she knew me before, the way I used to be. But that has to be my paranoia talking. I'd never seen her before my first day at Edgewood. I look away, listening for the sound of her engine to fade completely before lifting my eyes again.

Before I know it, I'm the only one left on the bleachers. I pull out my sketchbook when I get to the bottom of the stands, take a seat on the first row, and begin sketching the edges of the field. I have an idea about drawing it overgrown with wildflowers but leaving the soccer nets and scoreboard like they've been long abandoned, an apocalyptic wasteland, and as I draw, I wonder what more I can do to be as good, as *great*, as my friends.

I'm adding vines to the chain-link fence and bleachers in my drawing when I feel the weight and heat of another body beside me. I jump, startled a little.

"You waited," Zay says with a grin. He drops his bag in between his feet and leans back, stretching. He smells clean and boyish, like green soap and grass. Tiny droplets of water are beaded near his temple, a place he must have missed when he dried off after his shower. "Sorry if I scared you."

"Oh, yeah, hi!" I reply. "I don't know why I jumped like that. Was somewhere else in my head, I guess." I go to close my sketchbook, but Zay stops me, his big hand hovering over the page I'd been working on and pushing the cover gently back open with his wrist. He looks at my drawing, then back up at the field, then down at the drawing again. A slow smile creeps across his face.

"Damn, Tiny," he says. "I like this. You should add a tumbleweed soccer ball floating somewhere over here, like someone just kicked it. Use flowers for the black patches."

I smirk, imagining petals making up the five points of the spots on the ball. "Not a bad idea. And by the way, it's completely unfair that you're as good at soccer as you are at art."

Zay chuckles. "I'm tryna be like you," he says. "I see you owning in every one of your classes. Don't you take twelfth-grade Calc?"

I blush a little. "Yeah, but math and art aren't so different. They're both things that happen in my head. You got brains and this *body* . . ." I freeze, try to backtrack. "I mean . . ." I look away from him because, *oh my God*.

"Tiny," Zay says, but before he can continue, a few other members of the team spill out of the locker room and walk past us, reaching out to bump his fist. Some say, "Nice game," or "I see you, Thompson," or just "Okay, Z!" It makes me want to disappear because it makes the same unworthiness I felt with Mila earlier bloom in me again. How did I end up here? Sitting next to this kind, talented, hot guy?

After they pass, after the field is empty again and the world goes so quiet around us that I can hear Zay swallow, I turn to him. "Look," I say. "Sorry about that. God, that was so weird. I just meant—"

"Would you wanna go somewhere with me?" Zay blurts. "Not now, but like, this weekend? There's this thing I've been wanting to check out, but I've just been waiting for the right person to go with and . . . I want to go with you. I mean, if you wanna go with me."

"Oh," I hear myself say. I swallow, and this time I do close my sketchbook all the way. I try to push down my embarrassment as I shove the book into my backpack, so I can really hear what he's saying. "Where?"

"Can it be a surprise?" he asks, eyes bright and crinkled a little in the corners like he's up to something. His grin is as crooked as ever.

"Okay . . ." I say, starting to smile again.

"Bet." He rubs his hands together. "I'll text you the details on Saturday. But there was something else."

"Something else, huh?" I say. "You must be high off your win, all these shots you're shooting."

"Maybe," he says. He reaches forward and takes my hand, and I'm so surprised that I stop breathing. His palm is rough and big, but I like the feeling of my skin against his. I can't remember the last time I held anyone's hand.

Just then the lights on the field abruptly go dark, and we're shrouded in the pinkish gold of the day's dying light. I look up, taking it all in. The sun has just begun to set, and by the time I look away from the glowing sky, away from the sudden dimming of everything around us, Zay has moved a bit closer to me.

"I was wondering," he begins to say. He licks his lips and is so pointedly avoiding looking at mine that it makes me want to laugh.

"Yeah?" I ask, wanting to tease him now. He's made me forget my faux pas, the way I'm not quite sure if I belong with him or Mila or at Edgewood High at all. "What were you wondering, Zay Thompson?"

"I like you," he says with so much certainty that for a second I can't look away from him. It's hard to believe someone could say those words with the amount of confidence Zay just said them, with a firm voice and an openness I'm not at all used to with guys. His brown skin looks gilded in this light. "And I was wondering," he continues, his eyes unwavering, "do you like me too?"

I blink a few times too quickly, and then before I overthink it the way I overthink everything, I'm leaning in, closing my eyes, pressing my lips against his. Our mouths are warm, but he somehow tastes minty and cool, and I immediately want more. When I grab for his shirt to pull him closer, I can feel him smiling without breaking contact, which makes me smile too, our joy as brilliant as the light that was just all around us and exploding within this unexpected kiss. My arms float up and I cup the back of his head. He grips my hip, almost lifting me into his lap. And I think he gets it—that this is my way of answering his question; that this is my resolute *yes*.

Even as my head whispers that maybe I don't deserve him or happiness or anything good, my heart hopes I'm wrong.

Jordyn be pretending.

That's all I think every time I see her stupid face. Pretending to be good. But she the biggest fraud I ever met. She be sitting there with her new friends, her new boy, and pretending that she so thoughtful and sweet and kind. She out here arguing with teachers and post- ing about protests and standing up for people, like she actually give a crap about something other than herself.

But it's all so damn fake. She only a good person when people be watching her. That's how I know none of it's real. Everybody else need to know the truth too.

But I do wonder how she doing it—how she can take notes and eat her lunch like everything all good. How she can laugh and talk and flirt like she ain't a life- destroyer. I don't get how someone like her can sleep at night knowing how many lives she ruined. We gonna be dealing with the mess she helped make forever. But she moved on like it never happened.

Maybe she ain't pretending. Or maybe she just tryna to fake it till she make it. It being a change. It being her becoming a better, less terrible person. Maybe she really do wanna be different. Hell if I know.

But why do she get a second chance? Who decided she deserved one? I wanna know how she is, WHO she is, when nobody looking. And I know how I can find out.

# 6

"You're home late," my mom says when I walk in, and her face looks like the eyeball emoji, like she's waiting for an explanation and it better be a good one. My skin prickles a little. We just got back to a good place, but her expression makes me wonder if my mom is already expecting the worst from me again.

Auntie Romy is sitting at the kitchen counter too, already sipping a cup of tea. She speaks next. "Yeah, boo. I thought detention was over yesterday?"

"I went to that soccer game, remember?" I reply, before dropping my backpack on the floor beside the kitchen table. Zay had asked me to go to a little victory party the team was having, but I told him I couldn't since it was a school night. I don't mention this to Mom and Romy, though I wonder if I should, if knowing that would help

Mom trust me more. I pull out my phone and I have a text from Zay already.

*Party sucks without you. But just to confirm, that means you like me too, right?*

I'm grinning down at his message when Auntie Romy says, "What you smiling about?"

"Oh," I say, tucking my phone into my pocket. "It's nothing."

She purses her lips like she doesn't believe me.

"I don't know much," my mom says, "but I know what my baby looks like when she has a crush."

Romy sets down her tea and smacks the counter. "My thoughts exactly, Jo. So . . . who is it?" She gestures to the pocket where I put my phone, then props her elbows on the counter and rests her chin in her hands, staring at me. My mom puts one hand on her hip and uses the other to pour me a cup of tea. After sliding the mug down the counter, she crosses her arms and looks at me expectantly too.

I take a sip, then smirk into my cup. "His name is Izaiah. Zay."

Romy lets out a low whistle, and my mom says, "Zay, huh? Is he in one of your classes?"

"Actually, we met in detention."

"Detention?" my dad says, walking in at the worst possible moment. "You like a boy you met in detention?"

Romy snaps her fingers. "Hey, Tony. Over here." My dad's disapproving eyes slide from me over to my auntie Romy. "If I may . . . remember the last time you jumped to a conclusion? Maybe we should let Jordyn speak before we pass judgment, or you could end up spoon-feeding her cake again."

Mom snorts and my dad chuckles, putting up both his hands. His quick surrender is what I love most about him—he never has trouble admitting when he's wrong. "You're right," he says. "I'm sorry, baby girl. Tell us more."

I tell them all about Zay—how he was only in detention because of a scholarship email he wanted to tell his parents about; how well he draws and plays soccer. As I speak, all three of them smile and Auntie Romy looks vindicated, because she sees she was right to be on my side the whole time.

"He wants to take me out on Saturday and wants it to be a surprise," I say, telling them about everything except the kiss. "He's really cute and a little shy. I think I like him too."

"He sounds lovely," Mom says.

"I usually think no one's good enough for my baby, but a D-1 college-bound athlete is . . . pretty good," Daddy admits.

"Friends who stand up to crappy teachers and a scholarship-earning crush?" Romy asks. "Looks like Edgewood was definitely

the right move. You're making all the choices I knew you could."
She lifts her mug like she's toasting with me, like she's saying *Here's
to you*. But what she actually says is "I'm so proud of you, boo. Keep
it up."

I nod and sip my tea, grateful when the conversation shifts away
from me. I scroll through Zay's art again, and then I smile when he
posts a photo from the party—him surrounded by the rest of the
team, grinning.

———

"We kissed," I whisper to Kaleb.

In Mr. Roderick's class, Kaleb and I have been mostly laying low.
No talking or using our phones. No note passing. We want to avoid
any further altercations with him since we still need to pass his
class, and he's seemed low-key pissed at us both since the incident
that landed us in detention and made him the subject of a school-
wide petition. We don't want to push our luck.

Roderick's whole demeanor has shifted too, and he's been keeping his red flag behaviors under control. But today I'm too excited
about my kiss with Zay, too pumped that we have a real date coming up in just a few days, to stay as silent as I normally would.

"Wait, what? Tell me *everything*. Paint the picture for me," Kaleb
whispers back, dramatically tucking his curls behind his ears like it

will help him hear better. "I want to feel like I was there. But, like, not in a creepy way."

I shake my head at him, then say, "I waited around after the soccer game. We were just sitting on the bleachers talking and he asked me to go somewhere with him, said he wants it to be a surprise, so he can't tell me any of the details yet. Then, like literally at that moment, the field lights went off and the sunset was making the sky this beautiful, intense color, and then he just comes right out and says he likes me and asks if I like him too. It was like a movie, K. So perfect that I kind of couldn't believe it. Then I just leaned in and went for it, and he kissed me back."

Kaleb lets out a low whistle, which unfortunately makes Roderick's head turn. "Have something you'd like to share with the class, Kaleb?"

"No sir," Kaleb replies quickly, without a hint of sarcasm in his voice.

Roderick eyes us both but turns back to the whiteboard, where he's explaining the weekend homework assignment—to create a simple logo for an imaginary app of our own creation that can be scaled to various sizes and still be recognizable whether a person is using a smartwatch, phone, or computer.

"So, what's next?" Kaleb asks.

"A date," I whisper. "At least, I think it's going to be a date. He said the surprise thing is this weekend."

"If I hear another word out of the two of you," Roderick's voice booms, "we'll have a problem."

I nod and lean back in my seat, away from Kaleb, deciding to be quiet for the rest of class and to give him the rest of the story at lunch, or at least after class is over.

"For example," Roderick continues, "if you were going to create a new logo for Tomcat Tea, you'd want to make sure it was a symbol that was scalable since you know you have a varied audience, including students, teachers, and staff."

A low rumble moves through the class. I feel my eyes go wide. "Oh yeah. You guys didn't know teachers listen too? I just listened to last week's episode on my computer, but I know most of you are listening on your phones. The current logo works great on my laptop, or tablet, but I'm sure it looks terrible on Ben's smartwatch, for instance."

I look at Kaleb, who frowns when our eyes meet. "So weird," he whispers. I nod, trying to reconcile this new information in my brain—that adults are listening to the pod too. I hope they're not taking it seriously, because if they are, it could be much more influential than I initially thought—could cause bigger problems than just rumors. My stomach clenches at the thought that Roderick might have known about my expulsion before he even met me, that he might have already decided I'd be a troublemaker. He might have even looked into what really happened at Hartwell. I avoid his eyes for the rest of class, doubling down on my decision to make my zine about activism. That could be a way to show him that I'm different now—that I'm trying my best to do right now even if I can't undo all the wrong things I've done in the past.

---

"It was just so messed up, the way they were talking about her, you know?"

Mila is saying this as I walk over to the lunch table, where I am the last to arrive. I know in my gut, without asking, that she's talking about Scarlett. I set my tray down and Mila gives me a small dimpled smile before she continues. "It made me remember how everyone was talking about Jordyn on her first day. How it could have been so much worse for her."

I know Mila must be really stressed and serious about this situation if she's calling me by my actual name with no trace of a joke in her voice. She reaches over and squeezes my hand. It takes me back to how I was feeling when I heard her defending Scarlett, how I felt when I kissed Zay. Like maybe I could be doing more to be better in some way—to be worthy of my new friends. Like maybe I *should* be doing more. And something tells me that this moment is my chance.

"I was afraid of that happening, actually. Afraid it would be worse. I came to this school for a fresh start, so having all the stuff with the podcast happen as soon as I got here was . . . scary." I look around and see Kaleb nodding and Anton frowning. Bryce shakes his head, and Mila touches my shoulder.

"I mean, I'm glad it wasn't worse. It seems like everyone has forgotten about me and moved on, but like Mila was saying, it is pretty messed up. I don't want that kinda smoke for anyone else either."

I debate telling them now about everything that happened at Hartwell—all the sordid details of the events that led to my expulsion. But if I want to be accepted by them, believed and trusted for who I am now, I'm not sure how much of the old me I can let them see.

Still, I take a deep breath and say something real, worried that if I don't, I'll fall back into my old ways of being—my old patterns of standing by or staying quiet. If I'm as honest as I can be with everyone now, and if I try, truly try, to make things better here for myself and everyone else, maybe the darker truths of what I've done won't matter.

"I've . . . always been afraid of being a victim," I hear myself saying. "I missed a lot of school when I was younger because of this thing with my heart, and when I finally went back, I was bullied constantly. I was small for my age. I didn't have the right clothes or shoes. I didn't know songs everyone else knew or about the TV shows they were all watching because I'd been in and out of the hospital so much. So I know what it's like to be where Scarlett is right now—to have people saying things about you because you're a little bit different. But I think there's something we can do about it."

They're all invested, as eager to do good as I am. And in that moment, I just hope the idea I have sounds as good out loud as it does in my head.

"What if we try to find the podcaster?" I suggest. "Figure out their identity and use it as a bargaining chip. Eventually shut them down? It has to be someone who goes here, right? It can't be that hard to figure this out. Plus"—I glance at Kaleb—"Roderick just dropped a bomb in first period."

Everyone looks at me.

"He said teachers and staff listen to the podcast too," Kaleb reveals.

"No way," Mila says.

"I know," I say. "It's so weird and stressful. It feels like they're spying on us or something, right? And, like, what if they take it seriously? People could get into actual trouble because of rumors that might not even be true."

Mila nods. "Figuring out who it is isn't a bad idea."

Bryce looks skeptical. "Where would you even start? If it was easy, I'm sure someone would have done it by now."

"Maybe we could come up with a list of people of interest," Kaleb pipes up, slapping the thick mystery he's been carting around all week. "To help us narrow things down."

"Ooh, can we have detective logs?" Anton asks. "So we can take notes? Oh! And maybe we could do one of those crazy bulletin boards you always see in police procedurals with black-and-white photos of the suspects and the yarn crisscrossing newspaper clippings and maps!"

I laugh. "I don't think it will get that deep, but if it does, sure. I mean, I guess you could always make your own bulletin board if you want."

Anton rubs his chin, like he's considering it.

Bryce looks around at us and sees that he's the only one hesitating. He sighs, but then he gets on board. "If you guys really want to do this, maybe I can make it one of my campaign promises. To find the person responsible for the podcast and convince them to stop.

Might be something to give me a leg up in the race since we know Peyton has the theater kid vote."

"Oh my God, that's perfect," I say. "I bet other students are as upset by Tomcat Tea as we are."

"Yeah," Mila agrees. "It was silly and fun before, with maybe the occasional piece of gossip. But it seems like now they're out for blood. I wonder what changed."

---

For the rest of the lunch period, we build our list of suspects.

Anton thinks it's a teacher, maybe even Roderick. I can see it because of how casually he talked about it in class. "And wouldn't that be just the cherry on top of his messiness?" Kaleb asks.

"It would be hilariously bad," I agree.

Bryce thinks it might be Peyton.

"Nah," Mila says. "She's way too popular. It's probably someone who doesn't have many or any friends."

"Yeah. I think it's definitely a loner," I add.

Kaleb thinks it could be a group of people. And we all agree that's possible.

"But I wonder what their motivation is," Mila adds. "Why would someone, or a bunch of someones, trash random students for no reason?"

I stay quiet, thinking about Hartwell. How the girls there operated. Why they did the things they did.

"It's about power," I say quietly. "Which is why I think it's probably someone a lot of people think of as pathetic. Or someone who feels pathetic for whatever reason. When people feel powerless, or like their power is threatened, things can get ugly quick."

"You say that like you speak from experience," Bryce says, giving me the side-eye like he wants to hear a story. But I don't take his bait. I shrug.

"It's not like this is something new. Powerful people have always wanted to stay powerful. Powerless people have always been mad about their lack. Both are capable of doing bad things if they feel like they're losing ground or if something scares them."

Everyone goes quiet, except Mila, who says, "Well, damn."

———

On the bus home, I text Zay about our plan.

*Our \*people of interest\* as Kaleb likes to call them include Roderick, a couple of seniors, Peyton Reynolds, and Scarlett Fisher.*

*Scarlett?* he sends back. *But wasn't she just on the podcast?*

I brought up Scarlett after I bumped into her in the hallway again. She gave me a dirty look, *again*. And then I remembered how she's seemed to hate me since the first day of school. How I could see her spreading rumors about people she doesn't like on a podcast. And like I'd said to my friends—I've been where she is. I know what it's like to feel like everyone is against you, and I know what *I've* been willing to do to feel a little more powerful in moments when I've felt powerless. What does someone like her have to lose?

*Yeah, but what better way to throw someone off your trail than by planting a seed of doubt by talking about yourself? Plus, wasn't she a student here in ninth grade, but away in tenth? Now all of a sudden she's back and no one knows why?*

*Damn. I guess that's true. But you could say that about anyone who's had their spot blown up on the pod. Even you, Tiny. Even me.*

Even though we're texting, I can imagine his crooked smirk, the way he might nudge my side with his elbow. It makes me smile and clears the conspiracies running through my head, but only for a second. *Oh please,* I send.

*Who do you think it could be?* I ask a few minutes later.

*No clue. But this person is careful. I bet it's someone you'd never be able to guess.*

Zay asks me to call him as soon as I get off the bus, but I wait until I'm almost home. He picks up on the first ring, and his face fills the screen, accented by that signature grin. I smile back.

"So, about Saturday," he says.

"About Saturday," I echo as I unlock my front door, setting my bag on the floor and leaning around the corner to peer into the kitchen.

"Jordyn, honey? That you?"

"Yep!" I shout. "Just on the phone. Be there in a sec." My mom is right where I thought she'd be, surveying the teas to pick out what we're having. I think I see her pull two sachets of mint green, and I approve. I head to my room, still smiling at Zay.

"Can I pick you up around five?" he asks. He rubs the back of his neck. "The place I want to take you is in Silver Spring, but I thought maybe we could eat before?"

"That sounds good," I say. "My curfew isn't until eleven. Not that I'm expecting our date to last that long, of course."

Zay smirks, his dark eyes shining, and then he looks away from the phone for a second.

I panic. "I mean, not that this is a date. I know we're just hanging out or whatever."

Zay looks back at the screen, and it feels warm and wonderful, like we're in the same room when he says, "Oh, it's definitely a date.

I was smiling at the thought of our first one lasting six hours." I laugh and cover my face. He chuckles too. "Worse things have happened," he adds quietly.

Once he tells me to wear clothes I don't mind getting dirty, and closed-toe shoes, I start to wonder what exactly the date will consist of. But it's also exciting to think about—that he'd plan something so involved just for me.

After tea with my mom, checking in with Auntie Romy, and finishing my homework, I go out onto my front porch to finish up Bryce's campaign posters. I pull out the two designs and add color, finalizing the zombies' shredded clothing, their snarling faces. I add Bryce to the second design, wearing his signature polo and untied boat shoes, standing on top of the slain zombies, a microphone in his hand, embodying his campaign promise of speaking up when it matters most.

As I finish the poster, I feel a vibration against my leg, and I glance down at my phone.

I grab it, wondering if it's Zay again, remembering some detail he forgot to tell me about tomorrow. But my smile falls away as I look down at my screen to see a message from a private number.

*Stop trying to be the hero, Jordyn. Stop making scenes and causing drama and putting your nose where it doesn't belong. Or I'll tell everyone the truth about you.*

The hairs on my forearms all stand at attention and my chest feels heavy, like something has fallen on top of me. I stare at the words, rereading the message over and over, not wanting to believe it's real.

*Who is this?* I send back. But no matter how long I wait, no new message comes.

# 7

The following day I'm on edge—anxious and jumpy around anyone who isn't Kaleb, Mila, Bryce, or Anton. I make copies of Bryce's posters and give them to my friends to hand out and post around school, but I avoid looking any of my teachers in the eye, and I don't speak to any other students more than I have to. When I see Scarlett towering over everyone in the hallway, I turn and head in a different direction, avoiding her completely.

In the cafeteria I'm quiet, while my friends are silly and loud as usual, and I even make up an excuse to avoid Zay when he texts asking to meet in the senior hall after lunch. In class I keep my eyes on my notebooks, my phone in my backpack, and my mouth shut tight.

Mila notices my withdrawal, because of course she does, and she pulls me aside in Physics, her brow furrowed, her voice soft.

"What's up with you today, girl? You've been so weird and quiet. Did something go down with Zay?"

I don't know what to say because I can't tell her about the text without needing to explain so many things I'm not ready to get into—Hartwell drama, big confusing problems, and everything else I thought I'd left behind when I transferred to Edgewood. I shake my head and give her a tight smile, remembering Kaleb telling me I have a great poker face after reciting those goofy victory speeches at Bryce's house. Mila is still watching me, so I try to summon that face even though I know I have to tell her something to explain my silence.

"It's just all this podcast stuff, I guess. Thinking it could be a teacher is really freaking me out."

It's not a complete lie, but it is far from the whole truth. The guilt of deceiving Mila hovers above me like a cluster of dark, damning clouds, but I don't know what else to do.

"Oh, is that it? You had me worried, Private School!" she says, squeezing my shoulder. "We'll find the sucker, don't worry. And even if it is a teacher, we'll take them down. I have faith in us. You should too."

I nod slowly. "There's something else too," I say, my heart pounding.

Mila leans in, ready to listen, and I clear my throat, which feels suddenly tight with emotion. "I guess I just haven't had friends like you guys since I was a kid. I haven't had people in my life who notice when I'm down or quiet for quite a while, and I don't think I've ever had friends who believe in the same stuff I do—who try their best to be good. To *do* good. And it makes me nervous, I think, that I don't belong with you. That I'm not good enough to be your friend."

I didn't know exactly what I was about to say until I started saying it, and as the words spill out, I know them to be true. I'm *not* good enough to be friends with them. I remember the things I said and did at Hartwell, the way I laughed and betrayed myself just to fit in, the countless people I made into the same kind of victim I'd once been. I don't deserve this second chance, this do-over, this new life. If that text message reminded me of anything at all, it was that.

"Oh please," Mila says immediately. "We're just normal people, Jordyn. Just like you. We're doing what we can to not make the world more horrible than it already is—just trying to break even out here and not make things worse." She lets out a laugh and I smile, watching her dimples and her dark, steady eyes. "I guess what I'm saying is there's no good enough. We're all just trying our best. If you're doing that, you're good. That's the part that matters."

I want to believe her. I want to take her words and hold them against my chest until my heart stops beating so hard and so fast, reminding me of my failures—reminding me of Bree. Until I can do something to bring her words closer to being true. Because the real truth is, she doesn't know what I've done. None of them do. But whoever texted me last night does.

---

Apparently a plan was made at lunch to go to Kaleb's house after school. I don't remember, probably because I was in a state of half-panic the entire time, reading and rereading the cryptic text from last night, but Mila swings by my locker right before I head to the bus stop and reminds me. Kaleb lives the farthest from Edgewood, in Upper Northwest with his grandparents, but he has a big garage where we can hang out without any prying parental eyes.

Anton and I ride with Mila, while Bryce hops into Kaleb's little hatchback with him. On the way, Anton and Mila argue about who should control the radio, while I doomscroll on my phone. I deactivated all my accounts over the summer and only reactivated when school started, muting and blocking a ton of people from my old school, but I'm starting to wonder if the unknown texter found me from posts other people still had up. For the first time in months

I search the names of a few of my former classmates to see what, if anything, they've been saying about me.

I don't find much.

Elise hasn't mentioned me at all and had only posted a few photos with me during the two years we'd been friends. Those, it seems, have already been erased, and while I'm not surprised by the fact that she so easily deleted me, it still stings. Lilliana and I were never super close, so I'm surprised that she's included a photo with Elise, Yasmine, her, and me on a post with the caption *the glow up is real*. When I swipe to the next photo, I'm obviously not in it. But the three of them look so different—older, with different haircuts, and Lilly's gotten her braces off. It looks like Yasmine hasn't posted anything in over a year, the last video being one of her and Elise dancing last summer. Lilly's post doesn't seem like enough to elicit a threat, but maybe it reminded someone of my existence. I'm surprised by how quickly seeing the three of them stirs up a tendril of anxiety in me that spirals like a long fuse. Unchecked, it could lead to an explosion that might include panic attacks or the heavy depression that nearly destroyed me over the summer.

My throat goes tight and my palms get clammy as suddenly I'm back in the girls' bathroom at Hartwell, back in the student parking lot, the gym and locker room, or the pool where I had my sixteenth birthday party. I'm ping-ponging through all the places where things went left and my world turned dark.

"Did you hear me, New Girl?" Anton yells. The windows are all down, and wind is pouring in all around us, plus the music is up—loud. I hadn't even noticed.

"Huh?" I ask.

"I said, do you know this song?" Anton shouts again, turning to look at me from the front seat.

I listen for a second, then shake my head. "It's a bop though," I acknowledge.

"Hell yeah, it is," Anton shouts. He leans over and scream-sings the chorus in Mila's ear.

"I'm gonna murder you," Mila shouts back, and I shake my head at them, trying to root myself to the fun, nice, neat here and now.

Kaleb's garage is full of junk. There's an old pullout couch, a half dozen card tables, at least twenty metal folding chairs, and piles of unlabeled boxes. The shelves along the walls are filled with a bunch of broken clocks and clock parts, gears and coils and detached second hands. I find a mesh umbrella stand full of maps on its side under a coffee table and an empty aquarium on top of a beach chair.

There's a corner full of tools and garden benches, a mini fridge Kaleb opens and tosses each of us a can of Coke from, and, inexplicably, a full-size mannequin.

"Kaleb," I say, as I look around and take it all in. This level of weirdness is just what I needed to snap out of the funk I've been in all day. I turn back to face him, amused, amazed, and a little afraid. "I mean this with all the kindness in my heart but, boo, what the hell?"

Bryce, Mila, and Anton crack up, because they've been here before and have had this moment already.

"I know," Kaleb says. "I guess I could have warned you. My nan is a bit of a hoarder, and my pop can fix pretty much anything. She finds old crap and my grandpa promises to fix it. Sometimes he does, but most of the time he doesn't, and it just lands in here for months. Or years."

"Yikes," I say. I pick up half a yo-yo and then put it back down.

"Yeahhh," Kaleb says. He shrugs.

Bryce ceremoniously clears his throat. "Okay, enough show-and-tell. Let's do what we came here to do," he says, taking charge the way he always does.

Kaleb drags a giant whiteboard out from somewhere I don't see because I'm too preoccupied by a jumble of faux pearl necklaces on the bottom of the shelf closest to me. I bend to scoop them up, enjoying the round slipperiness of the beads, the soft clicking sound they make as I move them around in my hands. I attempt to untangle the knotted necklaces while everyone around me shouts the names of all our suspects, and Kaleb uses a thick black marker to list them all on the whiteboard, which he's propped up against the wall. They all brainstorm ways to interfere with the podcast, find its creator, or stop its distribution, coming up with everything from writing a ton of terrible reviews to bomb its ratings, to flagging it for illicit content, to staying at school after-hours to figure out if it's being recorded in one of the empty classrooms in the evenings.

When I glance up, the list has three names, with notes:

Scarlett Fisher
• Loner/standoffish/doesn't have many (any?) friends
• Kinda mean
• Mysteriously disappeared from school only to reappear, during which time the podcast started

Peyton Reynolds
• On the newspaper, so knows how to write/tell a story

- No one would ever suspect her
- Knows everything about everyone and could get any info she wants because she's so popular

Mr. Quentin Roderick
- Red flags, red flags, red flags
- Brought up the podcast in class
- Seems to hate his students
- Knows technology well for an old guy and could produce something like Tomcat Tea

For a second I consider trying to stop them—telling them that this is a bad idea or that it will never work. But it was my idea in the first place. Besides, that feels like something the old me would do—protect herself no matter what the cost. Would someone interpret my part in this as me trying to be a hero? Could this get my secret exposed? I bury my fear about what could happen to me and keep my mouth shut.

As they talk, I sink back into the quiet I've been steeped in all day. I'm no closer to figuring out who texted me, but I also somehow feel even further away from my friends with this hovering above me. And I need them on my side. I've lost enough friends in the last few years that the thought of returning to that kind of loneliness makes it hard for me to breathe. The text told me to stop trying to be a hero, but how do I do that and keep my friends too?

"I have an idea," Mila says loudly enough that it takes me away from my thoughts and fears for a moment. "We're spending all this time coming up with ways to find the podcaster, when the thing is, maybe we don't actually have to find them."

"What?" Anton says at the same time as Bryce asks, "Huh?"

"Yeah, you're gonna have to explain that one," Kaleb agrees. Mila stands up and goes over to Kaleb's whiteboard. She erases everything.

"Hey!" he shouts.

"Chill. I took a photo before I erased it," Mila says, rolling her eyes. "As I was saying. What if we just make the podcaster *think* we know who they are?"

"I'm listening," Anton says, like he is the only one of us who matters.

"We can pretend we know who it is. Post cryptic stuff online about how the podcast will end soon because the creator has been found. Put up things around school. Bryce, you could even insinuate that you know something in your campaign posters. If whoever it is thinks we know who they are, they might give themselves up by accident. They might feel guilty, or start asking questions."

"So you want to scare them?" Anton asks, and when Mila nods, Kaleb says, "I like it, I like it!"

"That's not a bad idea, Mila," Bryce agrees. "Probably the best one we've come up with today, to be honest. I wouldn't mind giving it a try. But what do we do if people start asking us what we know?"

"Well, we add them to our list of suspects." Mila points at me. "And we give them the Private School poker face."

"What's up with you, New Girl?" Anton says, his voice booming out of nowhere in that low way it can, like sudden, rumbling thunder. "You been being a weirdo all day." All their eyes turn and land on me, and for a second I don't know what to do. But then Mila comes to my rescue.

"Leave her alone, Ant. She's in her feelings about something that has nothing to do with this."

"Yeah, sorry, guys. I don't mean to be a downer. Just let me know what we decide to do? I've gotta go, but I'll see you guys Monday."

I grab my stuff and move toward the garage door. Bryce shouts, "Thanks for the posters, Jordyn. Let's talk about button designs when you have a chance?" I nod and give him a small smile, grateful I did at least one useful thing today. Kaleb stands up and follows me.

"You good, Jordyn?" he asks.

I nod and smile so he'll believe me. He hits the button to open the garage, and as the door lifts, letting in the chilly night air, he asks if I want a ride.

"No, it's cool. I can catch the Metro. I need some time to think anyway."

"Okay," he says, but he looks worried. "Text me if you change your mind and I'll scoop you from wherever."

His kindness makes my eyes prick, and I just want to get away faster. I give him a quick hug, wishing I could tell him more, wishing I could tell them all everything.

Kaleb's skinny, and his biceps aren't very impressive. But I'm so tiny that he easily lifts me off my feet.

# 8

Zay picks me up on Saturday evening just like he said he would. He's wearing a pair of stylishly ripped jeans with a bright blue bomber jacket and matching blue sneakers. He looks like he got another shape-up too, his hairline almost mathematical, the angles are so freshly cut. He looks good, like he took care to show me the best version of himself.

When he arrives, I'm grateful both my parents are working. Auntie Romy answers the door, and though she (embarrassingly) looks Zay up and down, she smiles broadly at him too.

"Hello, Izaiah," she says. "Her curfew is eleven, and I suggest you have her back closer to ten forty-five. Her parents will be home by then, so you won't have the cool auntie who would let you slide being a few minutes late." She does the double-point-at-her-eyes-point-at-his-eyes thing, like she's threatening that she'll be watching him, so I hug her goodbye quickly, dragging Zay behind me, back to his car.

Zay drives an old Toyota that's dark blue and a little rusty, but he tells me that it used to be his dad's car and that immediately endears me toward it (and him). "Her name is Cecelia," he says, petting the dusty dashboard. "But you can call her Cece for short."

He takes me to an old-fashioned diner for dinner. "I wasn't sure what you liked, so I thought this place would be good since they have everything."

It's one of those charming places with well-worn booths and mile-long menus, where they have all-day breakfast every day and unlimited drink refills. I like the way it smells—like syrup and coffee even though its nearly 6:00 p.m. I order chicken and waffles, and Zay gets a burger with curly fries, and we talk about everything from my dreams about art school to Zay's big family. We order pie à la mode for dessert—cherry for him, pumpkin for me—then we hop back into Cece and drive to the main attraction: the thing he wanted to be a surprise.

"I know you said you started drawing when you were six," Zay says after we park. We walk across the parking lot, heading toward a big warehouse. "But who put you onto it?" I can hear house music blasting like it's trying to break the windows open and other things that sound like actual breaking—huge crashes and big bangs and loud voices booming over and under it all.

I want to ask Zay what the hell is going on, but I know he won't tell me. I'll find out soon enough, so I just answer his question.

"Well, I was sick a lot as a kid," I tell him. "I was born pretty early and the complications of that kinda lingered." I don't like talking about it—don't even like thinking about it. Remembering the beeps and clicks of the machines or what it was like watching my blood flow through needles and tubes, the bleachy smell of the operating rooms or the scratchiness of the hospital gowns and nonslip socks. The memories always make my body feel weird, like I'm sick and helpless again. But something about the way Zay is looking at me, the way I can tell he's really listening in the dying light of this Saturday evening, in this mostly empty parking lot, makes me feel safe, and the closed parts of myself begin to ease open.

"I had to have a few different surgeries to fix some stuff with my heart. My parents would always take me somewhere after I recovered enough to travel, you know, Disney World, that kinda thing. But my aunt Romy, she'd always get me a gift. And while Disney World or LEGOLAND or, like, swimming with dolphins or whatever was fun, Romy's gifts were always things I really wanted and loved. After my last surgery, the one that meant I was officially done, Romy got me a sketchbook."

Zay reaches for my hand. He doesn't say anything, just holds it and squeezes it tight, and it feels like he's saying everything I want someone to say when they learn this about me—*I'm sorry that happened to you*, without pity. *I'm glad you're okay*, with something like hope.

"I had a feeling it was her, just from the way she answered the door."

I laugh.

"I got someone like your aunt. Someone who sees me. You know how I told you I have three sisters? Well, the oldest one, my big sister, Talia, she's the one who got me into art. I was an angry kid. Got into a lot of fights and stuff. And I think Tali could tell I had all this stuff stuck inside, that I didn't know how to let it out."

"Like feelings?" I ask with a smirk. "That 'stuff' is called emotions, Zay."

He laughs softly. "Yeah. That. Anyway, once I started drawing, the fighting slowed down a lot. And once my gogo got me into soccer, it stopped completely."

"I can't imagine you fighting anyone," I say. "You're so . . . I don't know. Gentle?"

Zay nods. "I think this is who I was all along. I just was too afraid to let anyone see it."

I want to keep talking to him, keep teasing out who he really is, but we're at the door of the warehouse. And when Zay pulls it open, the inside is chaos personified.

"Hey!" a girl at a desk just inside the door screams. She has to so we can hear her over the immense racket all around us. She removes the kind of noise-canceling headphones you see on construction workers or babies at concerts. "Name?" she asks.

Zay gives our names and she hands each of us a pair of head-phones like hers, plus two face shields, two rough pairs of work gloves, and hard hats. She helps us get everything on and then ush-ers us over to a door where there's a sign posted.

# WELCOME TO THE WRECK ROOM
★ KEEP YOUR WRECKING GEAR ON <u>AT ALL TIMES</u>.
★ YOU'LL HAVE 30 MINUTES INSIDE. WHEN THE TIMER SOUNDS, YOUR WRECKING TIME HAS ENDED.
★ WRECK STUFF!

"Oh my God," I say, looking up at Zay.

He grins so wide, his smile isn't crooked at all. "You ready?" he asks.

Inside the wreck room there are old computer monitors and big box TVs from the '80s, wooden chairs, glass tables, mirrors, ceramic plates, vases, and more. On one side of the room I see cans of spray paint, sledgehammers, and pickaxes, and on the other there are crowbars and baseball bats. A bassy rap song booms from recessed speakers in the ceiling, but when it ends, heavy metal with lots of screaming comes on next.

"Zay!" I shout, laughing, as he grabs a crowbar and immediately starts whaling on a printer in the far-right corner. When I realize where I am, that no one is watching me, and that I don't need to shrink here, I grab a metal baseball bat and beat the crap out of a typewriter until the letter keys are flying through the air and skidding across the concrete floor.

We go at it for the full thirty minutes, shattering plates against the walls, spray-painting the floor, and crushing old AC units until we're both out of breath, sweaty, and laughing so hard we're doubled over. I've never felt exhilaration as exultant as this, maybe because I spend so much time trying to make myself into what people want or expect me to be. Part of me knows I'll never feel this free again. It's the perfect date for two people like us—two kids who used to be so angry and so sick we couldn't function. But now here we are: strong and happy and almost healed.

"Watch the door. I want to take a few of the broken pieces home with me," Zay says as he stoops and picks up shattered pieces of ceramic and plastic.

"What?" I say, glancing back at the door we'd entered through. "Why?"

"I want to draw them. It'll help me work on techniques like shadow, shading, and irregular shapes. Also, don't come for me for saying this because it's kinda corny, but I like making art inspired by broken stuff."

"What a cheeseball!" I shout over the music. But in this harsh light, surrounded by smashed and splintered things, I see what he means. It's all such a mess, but we can turn it into something beautiful. I crouch and grab a cracked letter *T* key from the typewriter. The long bit of metal that once made it move is still attached. I slip it into my pocket, then go up on tiptoes to kiss Zay in the middle of the mess we made together.

Hey there, Tomcats, welcome back! It has been another tea-filled week. Don't worry if you haven't been in the loop, I've got you. Let's kick off this episode with another one of our weekly recaps.

The Drama Club's first play of the year will be *Into the Woods*, and if Peyton Reynolds goes out for the lead, she is almost guaranteed to land it, though newbies Raylee Thompson and Emma Chester are hopeful as well. One thing we know about Miss Reynolds is when she wants something, she almost always gets it. Watch out, Raylee and Emma! Will she have time to do both the play and student government? That's for the voters to decide.

Today's tea is so piping hot, let me stop yapping and get straight to it. Make sure you're sitting down for this one!

Former besties Stacey Truman and Nicole Warith were seen arguing at the CityCenter mall this past weekend. The fight erupted when Nicole confronted Stacey in the middle of her shift at the Pretzel Hut over her being seen kissing Tre Navel! Turns out that Tre's been playing more than just second saxophone in the concert band—he's been playing both girls! Not going to lie, fighting over a boy feels a bit like the shenanigans from an overrated early 2000s teen drama. Low-key, that's embarrassing. Especially if the boy is Tre Navel, no shade. While we do love drama, I honestly hope the girls can reconcile and not let some dusty boy get in the way of a possible true friendship. Although I don't know if real friends would fight over a boy in the first place . . . but I digress. Let me know your thoughts.

Time for the BOMBSHELL of the week! We all know beloved soccer star Zay Thompson, the one I was just praising on our last episode, right? Well, I got ahead of myself. Edgewood's own Icarus has flown too close to the sun. Not only has it come to light that he's a massive player who has cheated on every girl he's gone out with—even the golden girl Peyton Reynolds—but it looks like Scarlett isn't the only potential felon here at school. Word on the street is that Zay is using performance-enhancing drugs, among others as well. Apparently someone saw him do a little something suspicious before the game. There's more to this story, but I believe Mr. Thompson should tell you himself. He really should care to explain why he's so cool with potentially putting the championship and his own future on the line. I really wish this weren't true, but unfortunately, it seems like it is.

Well, that concludes this week's episode. If you see Zay in the halls, give him some advice . . . or the number to a therapist. Your choice. Stay messy!

# 9

"Izaiah Thompson, please report to the main office."

I texted Zay as soon as I listened to the podcast on the way to school this morning, but he hasn't responded. I had a feeling his phone was probably blowing up, notifications stacking up like a block tower, so I didn't bother texting again. Still, I hadn't expected this: his name being announced like a warning over the intercom demanding his presence in the office during first period. I turn in my seat to look at Kaleb, but I don't say anything because we're in Roderick's class. Kaleb stretches his eyes wide, making his long, curly lashes nearly touch his eyebrows. *No way it's about the pod*, he mouths, and I want to believe him. Zay could be being called to the office for any number of reasons, but what if . . .

When I heard the pod spilling about Zay as if it were fact, I immediately felt an ache in my chest. Because whether it's true or not, I'm convinced he's being targeted because of me. Conveniently, I'd been able to forget about the creepy message I got on Thursday for the whole weekend thanks to the date with Zay and the subsequent nonstop text conversation we've been in ever since, but now I pull it up on my phone, reading the words again with beads of sweat suddenly prickling my temples: *Stop trying to be the hero.*

Is this message from the podcaster or was it sent by one of their sources? Does the podcaster know about Zay and me somehow? What if they saw us hanging out or kissing after the soccer game and now they're messing with him to get to me?

My phone vibrates in my hand, and I tuck it under the cover of my notebook so Roderick won't see. I open my messages hoping to see Zay's name. But instead, the new message is from Kaleb.

*I can see you panicking from all the way over here. Relax. We don't know anything yet.*

I swallow hard and nod, trying to believe him.

Though I don't think he'll answer, I panic-text Zay again.

*You okay?*

No reply comes.

At lunch, Mila has news.

"So Sara, who was in the office trying to change one of her classes this morning, heard admin talking about Zay."

"What did they say?" I ask immediately.

"It wasn't about the pod, was it?" Kaleb asks. He puts his hand on my shoulder. "I told Jordyn that it could be about anything."

"It *was* about the podcast," she says sadly. "Sara said they were all talking about how the coach heard about the podcast from one of the other players on the team—"

"Probably a benched player jealous of Zay's skills," Anton says, frowning. "I have photos of all those suckers, and I bet—"

"Anton. Focus," Mila says.

"My bad."

"So anyway, the coach listened this morning and 'has some concerns.' I guess they called Zay into the office to call his parents. They want to give him a drug test."

"Which makes sense, right? They'll test him and it'll come back negative, and it'll be okay?" I ask.

"I hope so," Mila says.

"Me too," say Kaleb, Bryce, and Anton all at the same time.

For the rest of lunch, we talk about our plan to catch the podcaster with a new sense of urgency. Mila says she'll start posting as if she knows who he is, and Bryce promises to do the same in his campaigning efforts. Anton says he'll stay after school on Friday to see if anyone is lingering in the computer lab since he can say he's editing photos, and he'll keep an eye out for anyone editing audio. Kaleb wants to do some digging within the episodes. He says he'll try to listen to as many episodes as he can to look for patterns in the way the person speaks. "Even with a disguised voice, there's still diction, cadence, and other things that could help us figure this out." He picks up the book he's reading this week, a contemporary story with two girls on the cover. "I can recognize my favorite authors just by the way their characters talk, or the way they describe stuff, and I bet we can do the same if we listen to Tomcat Tea more closely."

I tell them I'm too worried about Zay to think about how I can contribute, but that I'd love to be available for anyone who needs help. "For now I'm just gonna go look for Zay. Maybe he's already been tested, and this will all go away as quickly as it's blown up."

But after lunch, before I can even walk over to the senior hall where Zay's locker is to see if he's there, a notification pops up on my phone.

ZAY: *Hey. Not okay. They wanna give me a drug test, which I'm down to take. But my dad won't consent.*

*WHAT*, I send back. *Why not?*

*He says they don't have grounds to request it based on a rumor. That they should have concrete evidence to get additional testing done outside of the standard tests they require at the start of the season. And since I'm not 18, I can't do it without his permission. I'm freaking out.*

I don't know what to tell him. *Is there anything I can do to help?*

*I know you and your friends are looking into who could be responsible for the podcast, so you're doing a lot already. And I know you have Peyton as one of the suspects. I didn't tell you this before but she and I used to date. And I did cheat on her.*

I stop walking. I stare at my phone like I've never seen it before because this could be pretty convincing evidence that Peyton is the podcaster. I know I have to tell my friends, but will that betray Zay? And then there's me. I really like him, but can I really trust him with my imperfect heart, my flawed past, and all the ways I'm broken, when he cheated on Peyton, who everyone says is nearly perfect? Something sharp and intense jabs me in the chest. It feels the same way it did when Elise was triggered or angry and would become the worst version of herself. I'd feel afraid and unmoored, unsure of if I was safe from her wrath. The flawless image I had of Zay in my mind falls away bit by bit, like a sandcastle, and I wonder if I know him at all.

*I don't think she's the podcaster, but I didn't want you to find that out from anyone else. And look, I want to talk to you more about all this. But I gotta go.* Zay sends this message while I'm still trying to figure out how I feel about everything I've just learned. *I'll try to find you after school.*

I'm not sure how to respond. I don't want him to feel alone, but I can't betray my own feelings. In the end I send him a string of emojis that I hope come across as supportive, but it feels flimsy in the midst of what he's going through. I open the group chat to tell Mila, Kaleb, Anton, and Bryce about what I've just learned about Peyton and Zay, but I hesitate before I send a word, pocket my phone, and decide I need to think about all of it—the damning evidence against Peyton, and that Zay may not be as trustworthy as I initially thought—a bit more before I say anything to anyone.

---

Instead of Zay finding me after school, I find him. I head to the parking lot as soon as my last class is dismissed and I stand by Cece, determined to wait for him indefinitely.

After about twenty minutes, he materializes, but instead of a sweet, crooked smile on his face, his brow is furrowed, his hands stuffed deep into his pockets. When he sees me waiting, he softens a little, but not much.

I reach up to hug him, despite my conflicting feelings. He squeezes me tight.

"How you holding up?" I ask.

The guilt at the role I may have played in this situation is eating me alive, but he has things to answer for too.

"I don't know. I think I know who told Coach Carter about the podcast, and this morning I wanted to beat his ass. But honestly, that doesn't even matter anymore. I just got an email that my scholarship to UPenn is under review."

"No," I say, my mouth falling open though my throat goes tight. "You have a full ride. They can't be willing to let go of a star player because of a silly rumor on a tiny, stupid podcast. How did they even find out?"

"No clue, but these schools watch you like a hawk once they offer you money. It's crazy. I think they're less upset about the rumor and more about the not consenting to the test thing. But my dad is stubborn, and in his head, he's decided that this is harassment. He wants to fight it. And to be honest, I see his point."

I shake my head. "But a test would clear everything up so quickly. They're gonna think you have something to hide if you don't do it."

Zay shrugs. "My dad said that if they're testing me, they should test the whole team. At first Coach refused, but the more my dad pushed and pointed out that testing everyone was only fair, he finally said okay. So now anyone on the team who's not eighteen yet has to get written permission to be tested from their parents."

"Wow," I say. "This went from zero to a hundred in a few hours."

"Yeah," he says. "I bet my house is chaos right now. My dad's probably on a conference call with every lawyer he knows. My mom's probably crying. Gogo is probably stress-cooking, and Talia is probably stress-cleaning." His dark eyes are glassy, studying my face so intently that I can tell he's thinking about the other thing he revealed to me—the part that *is* true and has me questioning everything.

"I know this is a lot, and I know I owe you an explanation," he says slowly. "But can we maybe get out of here first?"

When I nod, we climb into Cece and I give him directions to Bread & Butter.

My dad's restaurant sits on a busy corner in the heart of Downtown DC, which means he gets all the tourist traffic from people visiting the National Mall, the Washington Monument, and the dozens of art and history museums, which is great for word of mouth. He's been covered in travel blogs and by food magazines and websites, and people are always tagging the restaurant and him on social media. But his favorite part of his business is his few but faithful regulars, one of whom is me.

Parking is nearly impossible in this part of the city, but we snag a metered spot for Cece after driving around for fifteen minutes right as someone else pulls out. As we walk the two blocks back to the restaurant, I tell Zay all about Bread & Butter to keep his mind off everything else. Talking also helps me not to spiral too much. After what happened at Hartwell, I want to run at the first sign that someone isn't a good person, but that impulse is at war with doing the right thing and not abandoning Zay in his moment of need— especially if I'm at fault for him being targeted.

"So, it's a soul food restaurant," I say as we walk along the clean sidewalks in tandem. The air smells crisp and earthy, like rain. "I helped my dad develop the menu, in that I lend my taste-testing services as often as I can."

Zay laughs and grabs my hand, and I swing it in a cheesy, exaggerated way to make him laugh more.

Inside, I wave to the hostess and head straight for the bar. Zay looks around and points out the murals that run along the left wall, the herb garden bursting from mounted clay pots on the right, and the three rectangular skylights in the ceiling that let in lots of sun. He rubs his big brown hands down the cool, dark wood of the bar. "This place is nice," he says.

I grin. To the bartender I say, "Hey, Chlo, my dad around?"

Chloe smiles and nods before filling up two glasses of water for us and sliding over a couple of menus. "Lemme go grab him," she says.

"What's your favorite thing to order?" he asks, scanning the menu.

"My favorite appetizers are the shrimp-and-grits bites. They bake the grits in a mini muffin tin with a single shrimp on top and then you get these cute little bite-size versions of the entrée." I slide my finger down the list and point it out.

"For a main, I love the sweet tea fried chicken. Instead of a regular brine, we use this lemony sweet tea recipe my granddad used to make every summer, and we add a bunch of herbs. Soooo good. Best side is a tie. If you're in a savory mood, I recommend the red beans and rice. Want something sweet? Go for the candied yams— we make them with marshmallows, cinnamon, and a little cocoa powder so they almost taste like s'mores."

"I'm bouta be too full to drive home, ain't I?" Zay says.

"If we're doing things right," my dad replies, stepping out of the back and materializing in front of us. He grins wide, shifting the shape of his salt-and-pepper goatee. "Hey, baby girl," he says, leaning over the counter to plant a kiss on my forehead. To Zay he says, "Anthony Jones," and reaches out his wide hand.

"Nice to meet you, sir. I'm Izaiah Thompson. Zay for short."

He takes our order and puts in the ticket right away with everything I wanted plus a slice of the chocolate cake Zay noticed in a glass cake stand at the end of the bar. "Well, Zay, I hope you're hungry. You're also gonna need the corn bread. Obviously. It comes out in a little skillet."

Zay looks pumped, and I'm grateful I could do this for him even if it just keeps his mind off things for an hour. "On the fly for my baby, please," I hear Dad whisper to a waitress.

When my dad steps away, I turn to look at Zay full-on. "So," I say.

"So," he says. "I guess I can't avoid this conversation any longer, can I?"

I shake my head. I want to ask a million unanswerable questions: *Are you a good guy? Why do you like me? Can I trust you?* But I settle on the one that might help me best answer all the others: "What happened with Peyton?"

"We were freshmen," Zay says, letting out a big sigh. "Soccer tryouts were at the end of the summer, so when school started, I already knew I'd made varsity. What I didn't know was how intense practices would be, or what it would be like being the youngest on the team. I had the most to prove, so I had to work the hardest. By the end of September, I was already falling behind in some of my classes."

I nod and take a drink of water, gesture for him to continue.

"I got paired up with Peyton for tutoring. She was great, and cute, and so kind, so after she'd been tutoring me for a few weeks, we decided to go out on a regular date. Fast-forward a few more weeks, we decide to make it official. She's my girlfriend and everyone knows it.

"Now, I should be clear: Peyton was never that into me being an athlete. She's more of a bookish girl than a sporty one, so she didn't always make it to my games. It wasn't a big deal to me at first. But then this girl on the girls' soccer team, Priya, asked if I could help her with passing. She was getting in trouble with her coach for too many turnovers, I guess, and so she wanted to work on control. She came to my locker and was telling me how much she admired how I played, and calling out specific things that had happened in specific games, so I knew she'd been watching me. It really stroked my ego. I never complained about making varsity as a freshman because it's a thing that everyone wants and I didn't want to seem ungrateful, but it messed with my head. And here this girl was showing up and telling me I was great."

"I can understand how good that would feel," I say, because I can see it. A few of the dishes we ordered start to arrive, but because my dad doesn't come back over right away, I tell him to keep talking.

"Yeah. So anyway, I agreed to help her. And I sort of started blowing off Peyton to hang out with Priya more and more. Me and Peyton started fighting. Things between us weren't great. And one afternoon, I was talking to Priya about it all and she was being so understanding, and I just kissed her. I felt bad about it right away, but I didn't tell Peyton about it for weeks. She found out because Priya told her. Priya liked me, I guess, and thought if me and Peyton broke up, I'd get with her."

"Wow," I say, taking it all in. "So what happened with you and Peyton after she knew?"

"Nothing," he says. "That was the wildest part. She just . . . forgave me. We broke up a few months later just because we grew apart, but Peyton never, like, held what I'd done over my head or anything. She told me she would have appreciated hearing it from me, not some random girl. She told me that was the worst part. So that's why I wanted to tell you the truth about the podcast. To be honest, I should have told you the truth sooner."

I want to be annoyed, I do. I want to be able to write Zay off as a player, a person who can't be trusted. But his face is so open, and what he's saying does feel real. For some reason I feel like I can trust him. If I want this year to be a fresh start for me, why would I hold something that happened two years ago against him?

"Okay," I say. "Thank you for telling me. I get why you don't think Peyton is the podcaster now, even with your history." The way he described her reaction sinks into my bones: It's mature. Kind. It's what a good person would do. The podcaster, on the other hand, seems petty and resentful. Maybe even hurt. I think I agree with him that the pod isn't something she'd do.

To my surprise, Zay laughs. "I wasn't telling you all that to convince you she isn't the podcaster, Jordyn. I'm telling you because I like you, and I want to be worthy of your trust. I've messed up before, but I always try not to make the same mistake twice."

For over an hour, we eat, and talk, and laugh, and Zay loves the yams most, just like I thought he would. I tell him he can head out without me when we're done—that I'll ride home with my dad because it will make him leave at a decent hour. Zay hugs me goodbye at the door, and once I find an empty booth to hang out in until my dad is ready to go home, I do my homework before taking out my sketchbook. Instead of drawing though, I rack my brain for how I can help Zay, because now that I'm alone and not amped up on everyone else's energy, all our ideas about how we're going to stop the podcast feel flimsy—or like they'll take forever to work.

"He seems like a nice kid," my father says as he hands his keys over to Chloe to lock up.

"He is," I say, thinking about everything he told me, everything that happened today and how I hope it hasn't ruined his future. "He really is."

———

That night I get everyone on a video call to update them on what's happened since lunch and to strategize about next steps. I leave out the stuff he told me about Peyton, because it doesn't seem like it would do anything but complicate things further, but I stow it away in my own mind in case any other proof pointing to her as the podcaster comes to light. As soon as I tell them about the scholarship being reconsidered, Kaleb groans, Anton curses, and Mila says, "Oh hell nah."

"The good thing is it's just under review, right? That's like under investigation? It just means they're asking questions. If he's clear, they'll find out soon," Bryce says. But he looks as nervous as I feel.

"Who knows. But that's not really the point, is it? This pathetic, lie-filled podcast could ruin his reputation. Black kids don't always get second chances, Bryce," I say, pushing all my worry for Zay into the words. They come out biting and sharp, and Bryce looks away from the screen, like he's ashamed of what he said.

"Sorry, sorry," I say. "I know this isn't your fault. It's just so messed up."

I tell them that I've been thinking that maybe we need to do something bigger, faster, because everything we've been talking about so far could take forever. "And what if this is just the beginning? What if Zay is only the first person this has real-world consequences for?" They all agree with me, but we get no closer to a real solution.

Once I hang up, I pick up the broken typewriter key I took from the wreck room and pull out my jewelry-making tools. Doing things with my hands, like making jewelry or drawing, always helps me puzzle through big problems. It's like, if my fingers are busy, my mind is just occupied enough to wander in ways it wouldn't if I was just obsessing about whatever the problem is. Aunt Romy always says the head and hands are connected in mysterious ways.

I use wire cutters to separate the key cap from the metal rod that once connected it to the keyboard, before filing it smooth. I add a thin wire loop, twisting it around the perimeter so the *T* is encased in a small cage, then I snake a silver chain through so that the letter

*T* hangs like a charm. I think of the wreck room—the spray paint and broken glass, the rules on the walls and how I followed them. I remember Zay calling me Tiny, how I kissed him in the dark. I slip the necklace over my head, the beginnings of an idea taking shape.

I go to bed puzzling through it all. I barely get any sleep.

---

"Isn't Izaiah Thompson your little friend Zay's full name?"

My dad is watching the Channel Four news when I wake up, one of the rare mornings he's entrusted the opening of Bread & Butter to Chloe since she still has his keys from last night. I step into the living room, rubbing my eyes. Mom's still in bed because unlike Daddy, neither of us are morning people.

"What?" I ask. It takes me longer to process things this early. "You know my brain doesn't work in the morning, Daddy."

"Zay. Isn't his name Izaiah?"

"Yeah," I say, stepping into the kitchen and putting the kettle on. "Why?"

"I think he's on the news."

# HARTWELL ACADEMY
# STUDENT PARKING LOT
# 6 MONTHS AGO

Elise unlocked her BMW and Lilly stepped in front of Yasmine to open the front door. Lately Lilly was getting bolder, like she wanted to assert her place as Elise's favorite over Yasmine and she'd do whatever it took to make that happen. I thought Lilly might be doing it to keep herself safe—maybe Lilly, like me, had convinced herself she could avoid Elise's claws if only she could get Elise to love her.

Elise had been on a tear for most of the spring, ripping into anyone at any time, ever since her mother's accounting business had gotten very publicly sued for fraud a few weeks ago. It was on the news the morning of our biology midterm, the story accompanied by her family photo with her mother smiling sweetly (Elise's face blurred because she's a minor), and it was all over the internet too.

Her father had gotten served at school that same day, but refused to testify. Hartwell kids couldn't stop talking about it.

Unsurprisingly, Elise didn't do well on the midterm. She'd gotten a D and as a result, her father had taken away the very car we were all standing around until she "straightened up," hiring a buddy of his to tow it out of the student lot in front of everyone, while he lectured her about discipline and priorities. Since then, the sweet but rarely seen side of Elise had nearly disappeared. The girl who would lend me her earrings or buy us all lunch on a random Tuesday had been replaced by someone who rolled her eyes at everything, laughed in people's faces, and was crueler than usual to her enemies and friends. No one was safe.

She'd only gotten the keys to her car back that morning after acing the makeup her father had insisted the teacher offer her—an exception no other student had received. It seemed that either the public humiliation of her mother's scandal, having her car taken, or both, had made Elise meaner, if such a thing was possible. But Elise didn't even seem to notice how often Lilly fought to be close to her, how desperately Lilly seemed to want to impress her. Me and Yasmine, on the other hand, did. I glanced over to see Yasmine's eyes widen a little at Lilly going for the front seat, like she too was afraid she'd been or might soon be replaced.

Elise only had her provisional license, so technically none of us should have been climbing into her slate-gray Beemer. But we always did. As I popped open the back door, Yasmine came for Lilly's neck at the front.

"What do you think you're doing?" Yasmine asked. Elise smirked and reapplied her bright pink lip gloss, slipping inside the driver's side like nothing was happening. I froze on the other side of the car.

"I'm getting in. Duh," Lilly intoned. She stepped inside, sat down, and leaned forward to grab the passenger door handle, but Yasmine moved into the space between Lilly and the open door, stopping Lilly's attempt to close it.

"I know it's been awhile," Yasmine said. "But I always sit in front, next to Elise."

Lilly crossed her arms and didn't move. "Oh my God, Yazzy. Does it really matter?"

"If it doesn't matter to you," Yasmine said, "why don't you get out of my seat?"

Elise snorted.

I was worried things would go left between the two of them, leaving me to restore the peace, but before their little disagreement could get any worse, I spotted Aubrey across the lot. She was walking with a boy—Greyson Pierce. She had her head down, but even from where I was leaning against Elise's car, I could tell Aubrey was blushing.

I silently hoped Elise wouldn't notice Aubrey because I always hoped Elise didn't notice Aubrey. But I especially hoped Elise didn't notice her today since she was with Greyson, Elise's ex.

I spoke up, hoping to keep Elise's attention on our friends. "Yasmine, you always sit up front. Maybe you should just let Lilly have a turn?"

Yasmine looked over at me like I'd betrayed her, but Elise piped up next. "Yeah, Yaz. Just let Lilly sit here. Anyway, I wanna get out of this dump. It's the freakin' weekend."

"But I always ride shotgun with you," Yasmine whined. "I have since you first got your learner's permit."

"Who cares?" Elise said. And I agreed, quickly, silently willing Aubrey to walk faster or at least to walk away from Greyson. "Yeah," I said. "Just get in so we can go?" I glanced from Elise to Aubrey and back again before I could stop myself.

Elise squinted at me, then seemed to follow my eyes to where Aubrey and Greyson were standing. Lilly and Yasmine were still bickering, but I wasn't listening to them. I was waiting and watching Elise. And when Elise slipped on her sunglasses and popped open her door, I knew things were about to get ugly.

As an only child, Elise wasn't good at sharing—things or people. And once she'd decided someone was hers, no one else got to have them. It was why I felt stuck with Yasmine and Lilly, why I knew I'd never date Greyson, or anyone else at this school. There were too many boys who were off-limits because they'd once liked Elise, or kissed Elise, or because Elise had had crushes on them when they'd been pimply middle schoolers. And I'd decided a long time ago that Elise's Do Not Touch list was too sprawling for me to keep track of, the consequences of breaching the invisible contract too great. So, I didn't date Hartwell boys. I barely looked at them.

Aubrey, however, clearly didn't know about the List of Boys Elise Had Claimed. She didn't know the rules. She hadn't been a student at Hartwell as a freshman, so she probably didn't even know Greyson was Elise's ex-boyfriend. To add insult to injury, Aubrey had gotten the highest score in the class on our biology midterm. So the second Elise laid eyes on Aubrey, I knew she was out for blood.

"Hey, Grey," Elise said, leaving me with the still-arguing Yasmine and Lilly at her car. I watched as she crossed the lot, closing the distance between them slowly. They were just close enough for me to hear every word they said.

"'Sup, Elise," Greyson said. He tucked his fingers into his pockets and rocked back on his heels. "Got your car back, huh?" he asked.

Elise twirled her hair and grinned. "Yep. Daddy had it washed and waxed for me too."

Elise glanced at Aubrey, who was, for some reason, still standing beside Greyson. I still wanted her to run—tried to tell her as much with my eyes. I willed her to move with my soul. "Bree," Elise said in a half-hearted greeting. And I cringed. Aubrey only liked her friends to call her that.

Aubrey looked up, her eyes surprised and scared, but just said "Hey" in her quiet voice.

"So, Grey, why didn't you tell me you were into her?" Elise said.

Greyson looked confused. "Tell you I was into . . . who?" he asked.

"Aubrey. I mean, you're walking her over to the bus stop, right? And she's giggling and you're smiling. You're totally into her, I can tell. Bree, I can totally tell. This is exactly how he would act with me when we were together."

Aubrey's hazel eyes went wide as she realized the mistake she'd made. And I knew exactly what would happen next, though I prayed I was wrong.

Greyson looked at Aubrey and laughed. "I'm not into her," he said simply, resolutely, but with so much apathy that it hurt me even from ten feet away. "I mean, no offense, Aubrey," he said, briefly glancing at her, "but you're not my type."

"Why?" Elise said, and I clenched my fists.

"What do you mean why?" Greyson asked.

"Why isn't she your type?"

Greyson glanced at Aubrey, and I saw his Adam's apple bob, swallowing hard because he knew Elise, so he knew what was about to happen. He also knew he was powerless to stop it. Just like I was.

I suddenly felt like a sick little kid again, sitting in a doctor's office, unsure of why my mother looked so worried, afraid that something else bad was about to happen to my body. My heart fluttered, the way it always did when I was excited or anxious. But this time, it wasn't myself I needed to worry about.

"She just isn't," he said. "Can you drop it? Your friends are waiting."

Elise turned back to look at us, so I raised my brows, begging with my eyes for her to come back. But Elise ignored me.

"Is it her oily hair?" Elise asked, reaching out to finger Aubrey's limp, dirty-blond locks. "Or maybe it's the combination of these crazy thick glasses and her terrible skin. Or could it be because she never speaks? Earth to Bree!" Elise shouted, right in Aubrey's face.

Aubrey turned her head away, nostrils flaring, like she was about to cry.

"Elise," Greyson said, his tone darkening. But she didn't care.

"Oh, I know! It's the way she smells, right? It's called deodorant, girl. Get some. Or maybe it's the fact that she never shaves her legs or her armpits. Which, now that I think about it, might be why she stinks." Elise pinched her nose and took a step back. Then she tapped her finger on her chin and circled Aubrey slowly, like a shark. "Or maybe it's the way she doesn't have any friends. Except teachers. And we all know they only put up with her because they feel bad for the scholarship kid."

That part stung. Both because Bree used to be my friend and because, in that moment, I caught Bree's eyes. There was pain in them, of course, but there was something else there too that was directed straight at me—hatred.

Yasmine and Lilly, who had stopped arguing to watch the exchange, let out low whistles.

And I watched Aubrey wither. I understood why she didn't fight back, because it was the same reason I wasn't speaking up—self-preservation—but I didn't understand why Aubrey wouldn't at least leave. It was the one thing I had told her when I found out she'd be coming to Hartwell—*You don't want to fight with these kids,*

*Bree. This isn't like it was in middle school. If something goes down, just walk away.*

Greyson didn't laugh, which I appreciated. He said, "Jesus, Elise," shaking his head and turning to go. As he walked away, Elise shouted, "I guess it makes sense that you're not into her. I should have known you wouldn't go from *me* to *that*."

Aubrey did cry then. And I couldn't bear to watch. I turned back to Elise's car, got in, and shut the door.

# 10

*Did you see?*

I send the text to Mila as I get ready for school, still shaking over the story about Zay on the news. The anchor's voice echoes down the hallway even now, and phrases like "fallen hometown hero," "once-promising future," and "performance-enhancing drugs" make me want to slam my door.

*Yeah*, Mila sends back. *I can't believe it. And did you see the picture they used?*

The story was airing with a photo of Zay from one of the team's victory parties, where he has his middle fingers thrown up, making a funny face. It would have been so easy for them to request one from school, or use his official roster photo, but I knew exactly why they hadn't done that. They want to make him look like he's the kind of kid who would do something like what he's accused of. They're spinning the story before anything has even been proved.

*I can't even deal*, I send back before I wrestle my hair into a puff near the nape of my neck. I smooth my edges, tie my shoes, and grab my phone again.

*I know you aren't close with him, but I have to do something*, I send. Since our meal and conversation at Bread & Butter, I've felt confident I could trust Zay. His vulnerability and honesty tore down the protective walls I'd mounted around my heart, and I instead want to protect *him*. I touch the typewriter-key necklace I made last night where it sits on my dresser. I feel the last few loose strings of my idea falling into place. I won't be able to do it alone.

*I'll need help*, I type, but before I hit send, another message from Mila lands on the screen.

*Any friend of yours is a friend of mine. Besides, you know how I told you that me and Kaleb were on the pod? Well, Kaleb was the very first victim. It's why he doesn't like to listen to it. I was the second. So this has always been bigger than Zay.*

This information lands unexpectedly hard, and I feel more confused than before about who the podcaster might be. I can't think of anyone at school who would have it out for Mila and Kaleb. And I can't even imagine what gossip anyone could have on them. Unless, like Zay, I've oversimplified them—made them great in my mind when there's more to them than that. I still want to believe that good people exist, that I can be a good person too, but I'm starting to wonder if it's possible for mistakes to make people *better*. I remember how Zay said that he tries not to make the same mistake twice, and as I realize everyone I know must have secrets, Mila texts again.

*What are you thinking?*

—————

"This just got real," Anton says.

He leans against my locker after I slam it closed, cursing under my breath because he scared me. I may be feeling paranoid because of everything I told Mila this morning, because of everything we're going to try to do. "I know," I say. "I called Zay this morning, and he's staying home from school today, too embarrassed to show up and so stressed about everything. None of the ideas we had before are going to work, but I have something in mind that could. It's risky though."

Anton smirks. "You're speaking my language, New Girl."

I tell Anton about my plan right there in the hallway, laying out exactly what we'd need to pull it off. "I don't know if it's too complicated to do right away, but I really want to do it tonight," I tell him. "Mila says she can get the spray paint from her cousin, so I'm gonna swing by her place after school to pick it up. I'll send you a few photos when it's done if you'll lend Frida to me. We can leak them online either tonight or tomorrow, early."

Anton nods and claps one quick time. He grins and grabs my shoulders. "We got this. Easy peasy."

In first period I tell Kaleb the details and ask if he's down. I need at least one other person with me, to do what needs to be done. "Um, duh," he replies, and then I can't help but remember what Mila told me this morning.

"What did the podcaster say about you, when you were on the pod? Mila told me the two of you were the first victims."

Kaleb glances up at Roderick, then back at me. He points to his notebook with his pen.

Kaleb writes, and when he rips out the page and hands it over, I can't believe the sentence on the page in front of me: *The pod outed me.*

*No way*, I write back.

*Yeah. I'll tell you the rest after class.*

As soon as Roderick dismisses us, I turn to Kaleb and say, "Spill."

He tucks his curls behind his ears and smiles a sad smile. We grab our stuff, and as we start down the hall to our next classes, he tells me everything.

"Okay. So. Here's the short version of a really long story. Me and Bryce used to be best friends. Like BFF besties. But then in middle school I realized I was gay, and I just felt like I couldn't tell Bryce. He was so bro-y sometimes, and he made a lot of rude, homophobic jokes. I know he wouldn't have done that if he knew about me, but still. It just rubbed me the wrong way."

I nod. "Of course it did."

"Fast-forward to freshman year of high school. We met Mila and Anton, and the four of us started hanging out. I immediately just felt closer to them than to Bryce. Me and Mila liked the same music, and Anton and I bonded over this sci-fi book series we're both obsessed with. So I ended up coming out to Mila, and then me and Anton started having these long video calls talking about books and movies, and we got a lot closer than we had been the year before. I came out to him too.

"Over the summer a bunch of kids from Edgewood started hanging out at Rock Creek Park on Saturday nights, and on one of those evenings, I finally told Bryce. Then he asked me if Anton or Mila knew—the two of them had walked to the little creek behind us where kids sometimes stashed beer, and we'd already had a few. When I said yes, he was all, like, 'Oh, so you told them before me?' and he started saying all this stuff about how we used to be close and asking why I'd pick them over him."

"Oh no," I say.

"I blurted out the thing about the jokes he used to make, and he was screaming that he was twelve and how could I hold that against him, and then Mila came over and yelled back at him that I didn't have to tell him at all, and Anton was all, like, 'Whoa, everybody, chill.' But yeah. That fight caused this big rift between us. The pod came out a few weeks later, and it's actually part of the reason we started talking again. At first I was upset with all three of them, convinced one of them told whoever had created the podcast. But when Mila was on it the next week, she pointed out that we hadn't been alone at the park. We'd made a scene with other people around, so who knows who overheard us."

"Wow," I say.

"Yeah. It sucked. But everyone here was mostly cool about it— the gay thing, I mean. I just wish I could have done it on my own terms."

I shake my head. I had no idea. "What did the pod say about Mila?"

"Oh, this super ridiculous thing about her youngest sister really being her secret kid? It was laughable. That's the thing that's so weird about Tomcat Tea. How some of it is true and some of it isn't."

I'd been thinking about that too. It's what makes the podcast so dangerous. "I think they do it on purpose. Depending on who they're upset with, who they want to flame, if they don't have anything real, they just make something up."

———

I'd been planning to fill Bryce in on everything at lunch, but after hearing how he reacted to finding out Kaleb was gay after everyone else, I was worried he'd flip about being the last to know my plan. I decide to drop the info into the group chat—that way by lunch everyone will be all caught up. Bryce is the last piece of the puzzle, so in the cafeteria we go over the roles everyone will play, how and why they need to do exactly as I say so it will all go off without a hitch.

"So, we all have our marching orders," Bryce says. "Kaleb, you can definitely tell your grandparents you're sleeping at my place. And as long as you're there for dinner with my parents, I can sneak you out after they go to bed. It's a flawless alibi, bro."

"Awesome, *bro*," Kaleb says, voice full of sarcasm. Bryce playfully punches him in the arm.

"Perfect. I'll be doing the same at Mila's since she has the spray paint. Kaleb, is this afternoon enough time to do what you need to do?"

He nods.

I think over everything, running through the details in my head. Without consciously deciding to, I remember what it was like at Hartwell. How alone I felt. How guilty. Almost every day I did something I wasn't proud of, but I can do something different now. I don't want to be remembered only for my worst moments, and I know everyone else at this school feels the same way.

If we get caught, my parents will punish me for the rest of my life, not to mention the terrifying possibility of detention, suspension, or even being expelled again . . . But this feels like one of those moments—a defining one where I can do something that makes a difference, or I can sit back and do nothing. The old Jordyn would hide, stay quiet, just try her best to survive. But this is Zay's future, maybe all our futures. I won't be a bystander this time.

"Am I missing anything?" I ask, and Mila shakes her head.

Anton says, "It's kinda brilliant," and Bryce nods in agreement.

Kaleb says, "Let's do it on the ground instead of a wall though. A parking lot is less likely to be painted over immediately."

I nod, making a mental note.

"So true," Bryce agrees.

"Do you think it will work?" I ask next, looking around at my friends. They all look at one another. And then all four of them smile.

"Hell yeah," Mila whispers.

———

The spray paint bottles ping against one another in my backpack as I step off the bus with Kaleb. It's nearly 1:00 a.m., and the streets are deserted aside from us. The wind picks up as I hand him back his phone, on which I'd been scrolling through the website he'd pulled together in record time. I called him to confirm what I wanted it to look like a little over two hours ago, and now we're outside, jackets on, seconds away from doing something that could get us both in serious trouble. I'm so anxious that I'm trembling, but I've come too far to turn back now.

"It's perfect," I say. "Is it live?"

"It can be, as soon as I hit publish."

"Do it," I say without looking at him, my eyes glued forward on the tall, shadowed walls of Edgewood High, where it stands like a statue, moonlit and stoic in the dark.

We head around to the side of the building. The parking lot is chained shut.

"Dammit," I whisper, but when I glance back at Kaleb, he gives me a single nod. We both grab a handful of the chain-link fence, scaling it and jumping down over the other side without hesitation. We scramble out of the way of the single streetlight that brightens the left half of the lot.

In the shadows, I pull out my phone, navigate to secretshurt.me, and type quickly, filling the white text box that floats like an island in the center of the otherwise dark page. I read the call to action, a single sentence above the box, before I press post.

*Share a secret, kill the pod.*

"We need to be quick," Kaleb says.

"I know. I just wanted to make sure it worked."

"You don't trust me?" he asks with a smirk.

"You know I do," I tell him. He pulls up the site again on his phone. Hits refresh. The words I typed are there, a first post on a page that has infinite room for more, anonymous but undeniably public: *I'm 16 and I still sleep with my baby blanket.*

"I'll add one too," he says. His curls flop into his eyes and he pushes them away. He types, hits post. And then there it is, right above mine: *I pissed the bed until I was ten.*

I read it and look back up at him. He shrugs. Says, "Don't judge!"

I say, "Would never." I unzip my bag and pull out a can of hot-pink paint. I toss a neon-yellow one to Kaleb.

"You do the words," I tell him. "I'll make it pretty."

We work silently, our footsteps and the hiss of the spray paint exiting the cans the only sounds filling the space between us. Kaleb paints the sentence we'd agreed upon in looping letters that look nothing like his boxy handwriting, and I come behind him, painting lips and a microphone and a listening ear. I add thorny vines and flowers with bleeding petals—because the truth can be beautiful, dangerous, and painful.

When we back away to take in the full mural, we look at each other, grinning.

## MY BIGGEST SECRET IS

## READ MINE. SHARE YOURS.
## SECRETSHURT.ME

# PART TWO

# OCTOBER

# GROUP CHAT

**KALEB:** *Jordyn, you up?*

**KALEB:** *DID YOU SEE?*

**KALEB:** *My phone has been blowing up with notifications from the site all morning. Had to turn them off.*

**MILA:** *Really?*

**KALEB:** *Yeah, look: secretshurt.me*

**BRYCE:** *Whoa.*

**ANTON:** *These can't all be secrets from our school. Right?*

**KALEB:** *I don't know. I kinda think randos are posting too.*

**ANTON:** *THIS IS CRAY*

**MILA:** *So many people have seen it already and we're not even at school yet.*

**BRYCE:** *Imagine when people see it IRL.*

**ANTON:** *Yoooooo. New Girl. This might actually work!*

**MILA:** *I can't believe this.*

**KALEB:** *Where is J???*

# 11

My phone is hot to the touch when I wake up.

I yank my hand back, surprised, and pull out the charging cable. I tap the screen to wake it up and see that I have over a hundred text messages, all from our group chat.

I read the first dozen or so with mounting excitement. There's more, but I've seen as much as I need to. I sit up and text my friends back.

Jordyn: *Holy crap. Is this real life?*

Mila: *I think it is, Private School. I think it really is.*

When Kaleb and I were done with the mural last night, I took a photo and sent it to Anton. He knew I wanted him to share it anonymously everywhere he could. He said he'd post it on street art photography threads he follows and across a bunch of the other platforms where he'd made burner accounts just for this purpose. I guess the links got picked up and made the rounds.

The idea was, if everyone's secrets are already out in the open, the podcast wouldn't have anything left to expose. With the protection of anonymity, I thought kids might be more open to putting their secrets out there. And if they weren't hiding their pasts anymore, the podcast wouldn't have the same power over them. Over any of us. Of course, the podcaster could always make things up, like they had done before, or arbitrarily assign secrets from the site to kids they decided to target, but with so many secrets populating the page, my hope was that they'd have less sting and would be less scandalous if it wasn't the first time anyone was seeing or hearing about various transgressions. Plus, the power the pod has right now is in its ability to expose truths people wanted to keep hidden. If *everything* on the pod was a lie, over time it would discredit itself.

I click the link and start reading through some of the secrets. People have shared everything from cheating on tests to cheating on their boyfriends, broken promises and other bigger ways they'd caused harm. Shameful things I was certain they'd kept to themselves until now, where they could speak their truth without fear of retribution. I'm surprised by people's willingness to be open, by the freedom with which they're letting themselves be known. This was my hope when the idea for the mural first came to me: doing something to make the podcaster feel powerless, or at least a little less powerful.

Without my deciding to share, my own secret bubbles up from the box where I keep it locked away in the back of my mind. My fingers hover above my phone screen, and I feel tempted to type out the words I've been trying to forget for half a year. I swallow hard and go back to the group chat. I send one more message before I get up and get ready for school.

Jordyn: *I hope this helps Zay. But even if it doesn't, I hope it at least gets the podcaster to shut up for a while.*

Bryce: *I think we'll see what it does soon enough.*

When I get off the bus and cross the street in front of Edgewood High, there's a large circle of students around the perimeter of the parking lot. They're all taking photos of the mural, talking about it, and staring down at their phones—I assume they're looking at or posting on the website. As I approach, I play ignorant the way we all said we would. I don't see my friends anywhere, so I stroll up to a group of sophomore girls, making sure I look clueless and confused. "What's going on?" I ask.

"Looks like someone got fed up with the podcast," one of them says.

"Yeah," another one adds, "and they decided to get aggro on main." They all laugh.

They part so I can stare down at what I already know is there, spread like sunlight along the ground. The words and images Kaleb and I painted are brighter, more prominent in the early morning light, and I could imagine what they might look like from an aerial shot of the lot—a neon smattering of color against the gray-black asphalt.

"Whoa," I mutter in a low voice, because while part of me is surprised by just how vibrant the colors are—they make a statement in the best way—something else is there too. In a twist I hadn't expected, someone has taken sidewalk chalk to the blank space left after "My biggest secret is." They've written "I was assigned female at birth."

And then Mila is behind me, eyes wide, her hand reaching for mine and squeezing it tight. Pretty soon we're all being shuffled inside by our teachers, being told that if we don't hurry, we'll all be late for the start of first period, but no one cares. Kids linger by their lockers, walk up steps slowly, hide in bathroom stalls. The mural is all anyone wants to talk about, and my chest swells at the hope that maybe we did it—maybe we've fixed something that had been broken at Edgewood for years. A school where a podcast like Tomcat

Tea could get as popular as it's become must mean there's something in the culture here that thrives on drama, and maybe this mural can help everyone see that all kinds of gossip—recorded and broadcast or not—can hurt.

I follow Mila to her locker instead of filing obediently into Mr. Roderick's classroom. "Jesus," I whisper as soon as she opens the locker door and I can duck behind it to speak more freely. "I don't know what I expected, but it certainly wasn't this. I mean, I knew we'd make waves, but someone filling in the blank like that? I didn't see it coming."

"I know," Mila agrees. Then Anton is there, with Kaleb and Bryce not too far behind him. "The secret in the lot is definitely a big one," Kaleb says. "I bet whoever wrote it has been terrified the pod was going to out them, just like it outed me."

Mila shakes her head, and I mutter, "It's so messed up," trying not to think about how well I understand holding on to a secret that big, how it can weigh you down, color your every thought and action. "I just hope this doesn't backfire," I say, because having a secret out in the open is different from posting it on the internet. There's plausible deniability there, a level of anonymity that could never be re-created in person. "I hope no one saw whoever wrote it."

"I know we're not going to be able to focus on anything I'm actually trying to teach today," Mr. Roderick says, once he's finally managed to quiet the class down. "So let's just talk about what's on everyone's mind."

I glance at Kaleb because I can't help it. His eyes fly to mine, but go right back to Roderick in a barely perceptible flash.

"The mural?" someone says, and when I look up to see who has spoken, it's Scarlett Fisher, her voice cold and slippery as ice. "You can't be serious."

It's the first time she's spoken out loud in class all year, so everyone stares. Mr. Roderick leans forward and kind of smirks in Scarlett's direction. "Miss Fisher, thank you for your participation! And why not? This is a digital design class, after all. And I think the use of street art combined with an online element really upped the stakes of the statement they were trying to make, whoever the student or students were who vandalized the lot."

*Vandalized.* The word rings too loud and all wrong in my ear.

Before Scarlett has a chance to reply, a quiet boy named Jake with lime-green hair speaks. "I think it was activism," he says.

Scarlett rolls her eyes.

"Activism, huh?" Roderick asks. "Say more."

"I mean, it is an act of resistance in response to a form of oppression, right?"

"Oppression!" Scarlett scoffs. "Please. The podcast is not oppression."

Jake blushes but doesn't back down. "Maybe that was the wrong word, but . . ."

"I get what Jake means." This from a third student, a girl with braces named Grace. "It's someone deciding to do something to bring about change."

Roderick nods and encourages more students to say what they think about the mural, but I just keep my eyes on Scarlett, who is shaking her head and looking out the window, treating everyone like they're beneath her. I don't speak up for a while, because I don't want to bring any attention to myself, but eventually I'm so desperate to know what Scarlett could be thinking that I'm about to say something just to reengage her. Luckily Roderick beats me to it.

"Scarlett, I'm curious. Why do you think this isn't worth discussing? I would think, as someone who has been featured on Tomcat Tea, you'd be supportive of anything that could potentially topple its success."

Scarlett turns her attention back to the classroom, her eyes narrowing as she sighs. "I can't believe I have to say this out loud, but how do you know the person who painted the mural had good intentions? How do you know they don't want your secrets for some chaotic reason? Has it even occurred to any of you that it could be the podcasters themselves?"

The class goes quiet. And before I can stop myself, I say, "It wasn't the podcaster."

Everyone turns to look at me. Including Scarlett.

"And how do *you* know, Jordyn?" Scarlett asks. It's the first time she's said anything to me since the first day of school, and the coolness in her voice makes me want to shudder.

"I don't," I say immediately, hoping my face isn't giving anything away. "I just don't think it was."

Out of the corner of my eye, I see Kaleb, making a face that says *Shut up now, J.* But I ignore him because I don't want the whole point of the mural to be missed.

"Isn't it obvious that it's about more than the secrets? It's about everyone acknowledging that we all make mistakes and have things we don't want anyone to know, but that those mistakes, those secrets, aren't all that we are. I mean, isn't the point of the podcast to do the opposite? To make us feel shame for something we can't change? To simplify a person into a single story and steal all our complexity?"

Roderick looks at me like he's never seen me before, and even Kaleb blinks too many times, as if he couldn't have guessed what I was about to say in a million years. And I don't even think I realized that was how I felt until the words were spilling out of me, filling the room like the mural fills the back lot. Still, I worry I've said too much, so I shrug and look at my desk. When someone else speaks and my classmates shift their attention away from me, I do shut up. I say nothing else. But Scarlett watches me a little too closely for the rest of class.

---

For the rest of the week, all anyone can talk about is the mural. Students chat about it in the lunchroom and in the hallways. In an abandoned classroom, Bryce finds *My Biggest Secret Is* _____ written on the whiteboard. In art, Mila tells us she saw a girl mimicking the style of my thorny vines and bloody flowers that still swirl around Kaleb's swooping letters on the asphalt outside. In the girls' locker room, I find secrets scrawled on steamy mirrors and shower stalls, and Anton tells us he found the URL on white labels someone had printed and stuck on laptops in the media center.

On Wednesday, Kaleb notices someone using a hashtag when posting about the mural, and overnight it goes viral and I wake to Kaleb blowing up my phone with texts and screenshots. People across platforms pick it up, using #nomoresecrets, with hot takes about Edgewood, as the caption for cryptic photos, and in the descriptions for videos where they talk about how the hashtag makes them feel. Some people cherry-pick through some of the actual posted secrets, questioning if they're even real. The speed with which this is all happening takes my anxiety through the roof, and I wonder if whoever texted me before I got the idea for the mural is watching.

As the hashtag spreads, something else happens too: A new conversation starts among people way older than us hinging on how this isn't the first time secrets have been shared on the internet and that our generation isn't as original as we think we are. They claim we're repeating something that had already been done, and they make fun of how "kids" always think they're starting a trend when it had already been done bigger and better before.

By Thursday, half a dozen articles covering the mural and Tomcat Tea pop up on gossip sites, and even a listicle with the title "21 Secrets from a Small DC High School You'll Have to See to Believe." Bryce sets up an alert for the search terms *mural*, *Edgewood*, and *Tomcat Tea* to try to find any others, and promises to tell us whenever a new one hits his inbox.

I've been scrolling through all the discourse and online noise every night, and by the time I get to school on Friday morning, my head is spinning. Despite knowing about the mural's sustained and growing popularity, I'm completely caught off guard by what I see as I step off the bus in front of Edgewood High.

News trucks are sitting in front of the building, anchors holding on to their ties and skirts in the windy morning weather, microphones aimed at small groups of students all along the leaf-strewn block.

"Tell us more about this podcast," I overhear one of the reporters saying. "Had it ever caused a stir before now like it did with Izaiah Thompson?"

"How do the students feel about this mural? Have you seen or been a part of any of the conversations happening online?"

"Do you think the podcaster's actions were racially motivated?"

"As staff," one of them is saying to a teacher as she tries to move down the block toward the school's front doors, "how do you feel about the fact that this was happening under your supervision? It could be considered libel. What has been the school leadership's reaction to all this?"

I keep my head down, find Mila in the crowd, and pull her away from the chaos. "Oh my God, oh my God!" I shout-whisper at her. "What the hell is going on?"

Mila's eyes are wide and she's shaking her head. "I don't think any of us could have seen this coming," she says, and her phone chimes at the same time as I feel mine buzz in my pocket. She glances down at hers. "It's Kaleb," she said. "He's looking for us."

I go up on my tiptoes to try to spot him, but I don't see him anywhere. I do, however, see Anton. And he has a microphone in his face, a smile showing all his teeth as he speaks.

"Well, yeah, I mean, Tomcat Tea has been screwing with people for ages," he says. "I think whoever did this is really brave. I mean, they're always telling kids to stand up to bullies or whatever, but how often does that happen? And how often does it actually work?"

"I can't believe Anton is talking to them!" I say to Mila.

"I mean, I can," she says. "It's Anton."

"Yeah, but I thought we'd try to keep a low profile! I mean, we didn't *say* that, but I thought it was common sense."

Mila shrugs as Kaleb and Bryce come up behind us and nudge our sides with their elbows. "You went off in class," Kaleb accuses, a smile in his voice.

"Let Anton have his fun," Bryce adds. "You know the kid loves attention."

"I just don't want anyone to find out it was us," I say.

"This will probably work in our favor, if anything," Kaleb replies.

"We wouldn't want to be the only students not saying anything. That would look suspicious too."

I nod, agreeing that he may have a point. "We just don't know if this could turn bad. The attention is positive for now, but who knows if it will stay that way?"

"It is exciting though," Mila whispers. "That something we did is having such a big impact."

We all nod, and we keep watching Anton, and all the other students who have decided to speak to the reporters. They all smile and say so much more than I ever would.

All this mural business is cray.

I can't believe something this interesting is happening at boring-old Edgewood High. But here we are.

Half the school thinks the whole thing is ridiculous, but everybody else is into it. And a bunch of people wanna know who painted it. I got a couple ideas.

At first I was thinking Zay did it. Snuck in late, painted it, and left as fast as he runs down the soccer field. I mean, it would make sense—doing something like this to shift all that attention off him. And everybody know he always drawing.

But he's smart, so he was prolly laying low, trying not to get in any more trouble than he was already in. And if it wasn't him, it's gotta be somebody close to him—somebody willing to risk it all for somebody else.

I don't think the other soccer bros could do it. Seems like it took a lotta coordination and they ain't the brightest. If it wasn't him, and it wasn't the team, the only other person who makes sense is Jordyn. I peeped the way she be looking at him, and the way she was caping for the mural in class.

If Jordyn really did it, really put herself on the line like this, maybe she ain't being fake. Maybe she's finally decided to right some wrongs in the world.

Too bad she never made it right at Hartwell. And I ain't about to let her forget it.

# 12

"The team is agreeing to be tested. All of them."

When my phone rang Saturday morning, and I looked down to see Zay's name and photo blinking up at me, I nearly broke my nail, I tapped the screen so quick and hard to answer.

He's been out of school for a week, his father thinking it would be best to keep a low profile until the soccer stuff was sorted out, so he's been collecting and completing his homework assignments via email. I haven't seen him in days, and we've only been texting. I had been expecting bad news, so the first thing I say is "What?!" with a huge smile spreading across my face, relief washing over me like cool water.

"Yeah," he says. And I can hear the grin in his voice too. "Once they saw the news and all the articles about how Tomcat Tea wasn't always true and realized that things were getting real, Coach pushed and just about everyone got their parents to consent to their tests overnight."

"Zay! That's amazing," I tell him. "I'm so happy for you. Does that mean you'll be coming back to school? Not gonna lie, this week has been crazy, and I've missed you."

From across the room, Aunt Romy waggles her eyebrows. I poke out my tongue at her as my mom says, "Romy, leave that girl alone."

I slip out of the kitchen, where I had been having tea with Mom and Romy, and head down the hall to my room.

"When will you get the results of all the tests?" I ask him as I climb into my bed.

"I'm not sure, but probably in just a few days." Zay lets out a huge breath. "I really thought I was gonna lose my scholarship."

"I can't believe it had to get to that point for them to come through for you."

"I know. But I'm glad they did. And it's been a crazy week for you too? How come?"

I consider telling him that I'm the person behind the mural, but I decide not to. Not yet. I don't know what will happen next, and I don't want to risk connecting him to this when things are just starting to calm down for him.

"Oh," I say. "I guess you only know about what I've been sending you." I lean back against my pillows and settle in to catch him up. "You won't believe this, but reporters showed up at school wanting to talk about the mural."

———

I expected things to calm down over the weekend. Usually, these internet phenomena only last a few days, but it quickly becomes apparent that #secretshurt isn't slowing down at all.

A copycat mural at another school. A subgenre of ASMR where people record themselves in rooms so dark you can't see their faces, whispering their secrets and posting them to burner accounts. Graffiti on the sides of bridges and buildings.

*People are starting to ask questions though*, Bryce texts. *About who did this. I saw a post earlier where someone was telling people to give credit where credit is due, and to stop co-opting the hashtag, but the argument was brought up that the movement didn't start with the hashtag. It started with Jordyn's mural.*

We're all quiet for a while after he sends that. I'm silenced because he called it *my* mural, and that kind of ownership is not something I want to have to think about right now. The word *vandalism* cycles through my head again, and I wonder what the consequences for something like this could be.

*I think we should stay quiet for now*, I text. *Let this play out however it's going to play out.*

Everyone shoots me thumbs-up emojis.

*I wonder if there will be a new podcast episode tomorrow*, Kaleb sends. *I mean, the podcaster has to know no one wants to hear from them right now.*

*Yeah*, Mila replies. *This will be the real test to see if all this meant anything to the one person we wanted to shut up.*

The next day is Sunday, when a new podcast episode usually drops. And as soon as I wake up, I'm stressed. I spend the morning drawing and texting with Zay, anticipating a new episode and wondering who it might target, feeling anxious about the podcaster weaponizing some of the shared secrets, but there's nothing but crickets. I go over to Kaleb's in the afternoon and hang out listening to music in his garage, and while it starts out as a very low-key hang session, as it inches closer and closer to evening with no new Tomcat Tea, he says we should celebrate our triumph and "get the party started." For Kaleb this meant calling all our friends over to his place, and switching the chill music for something more upbeat with plenty of bass.

"Ding-dong, the pod is dead!" Mila sings, and we all laugh and dance, surrounded by broken things and a few that Kaleb's grandpa has made whole again, and feeling a bit like that ourselves: precious and worth saving, healed or at least healing. I know I'm not alone in hoping what we've done will save and heal other people too.

―――――――――

By the middle of the next week, I'm still in awe about how widespread our mural and its message has become. And when Zay jogs into the cafeteria, eyes shining, smiling wide, and heads right over to our lunch table, I brace myself for even more good news. It's a new feeling for me. I like it.

"The team's tests all came back clean. Including mine."

We all cheer. Anton gives him a high five, and Kaleb grins, and Mila says, "Damn right," while Bryce stands up and applauds. Zay playfully bows.

"Such a relief," he says. Mila slides over so he can sit down beside me. I squeeze his thigh and let my hand linger there. "But now," he continues, "all these places want to interview me."

I frown. Move my hand from where I'd rested it on his leg and ask, "Wait, why? What kinds of places?"

"Well, the Channel Four news for one," he says. "They're probably scared my dad's gonna sue them or something, so they want to clear the air. Feature me and highlight my 'accomplishments,' according to the phone call my mom had with someone this morning."

"How quickly the tides have turned," Mila mutters.

"Ain't that some BS," Anton says.

"Typical," Bryce agrees. "Trash the minority and then run a story calling them a hero a second later."

But I feel my stomach drop. "Who else?" I ask.

"A bunch of the same places that covered the mural, but I don't think I'm going to do any of the others. That had to have been crazy, right? Showing up to school last week and seeing it there? I'm kinda bummed I missed the big reveal."

We all get a little too quiet until Mila pipes up and says, "Yeah, it was totally nuts!" I'm worried my eyes will give something away, so I keep them on my pizza. But then I think about secrets and how they've poisoned the whole school, the way I did this for Zay and all of us, and that I did it to be a force of good. I also trust Zay, as much as I trust Mila and Kaleb, Anton and Bryce. So I just say it.

I lean forward and whisper, "It was us." Kaleb looks at Mila, who looks at Anton, who looks at Bryce. Then they all look back at me, grinning. I can tell they've been dying to tell someone, and Zay is the perfect person to confide in. "Well, it was my idea," I explain.

"And they all helped. But it was me and Kaleb who painted the mural and set up the website."

Zay's mouth drops open, then slips into a smirk. "Holy—"

"I know," Kaleb says. "We'd been brainstorming ways to bring down the pod all last month. Jordyn's idea was the best one we've had."

"And after all the stuff happened with you," Anton jumps in, "we were more motivated than ever to put a stop to it."

"There was no new episode, right?" Zay asks, and I shake my head.

"It feels a little early to proclaim it a complete victory," I say.

"But it seems like it may have worked," Mila adds. "Do you get to play this Friday?" she asks Zay.

"Yep. Now that they know I'm not doing anything wrong, Coach is desperate to have me back." He looks at me, and his eyes are bright with wonder or admiration, and something sweet and stickier—something thicker than like, but thinner than love. "You know, while part of me can't believe you guys did that, a bigger part of me can see it." He touches my cheek, then kisses me, and my friends absolutely lose it. I blush and hush them, and kiss Zay again.

And while so much seems right in the world, a small, skeptical part of me feels like it's all been a little too easy.

That night I invite Bryce over to show him the final poster design I created for his presidential campaign. With the excitement around the mural, I've fallen behind on homework, the zine, and the campaign materials I'd promised to help Bryce with—one last poster for his week of reaching out to seniors, and a few ideas for stickers and buttons. Now that a Sunday has come and gone with no new episode, and Zay is out of trouble, I'm trying to get back to normal life—to catch up on schoolwork and family stuff. I want to make sure I'm being a good friend too.

"Thanks for coming over," I say when I open the front door. "And sorry I've been so slow with this." It's the last week of campaigning before the election, so I expect Bryce to look tense or stressed. But when I open the door, he stands there wearing his backpack, chinos, boat shoes, and a crooked, mischievous smile.

"Oh God," I say. "What?"

"Nothing. Just wondering if I'm cutting into your personal time."

"Bryce, what?" I say again. "I invited you over."

"Yeah, but from the looks of it, you and Zay *clearly* need to get a room and—"

I roll my eyes and start closing the door in his face, but he stops it with his hand. He's cracking up.

"Kidding! I'm just messing with you, Jordyn." He keeps laughing as he walks right past me and into my house.

"My dad is still working, but my mom and aunt are in the kitchen, if you want to meet them," I tell him. "She made us tea."

"Tea, huh?" He grins.

After some quick introductions and Aunt Romy complimenting Bryce's gumption and ambition because he's running for president, we escape to my room to talk about his campaign. He thinks the last group of students he should focus on is athletes—that ever since everything went down with Zay and the podcast, the soccer team has been coming up to him and saying they're glad he's made finding the podcaster a part of his campaign.

"That's so great, Bryce! And the fact that there was no podcast this week has to look really good—like you may have really gotten them to shut up. Maybe the soccer players can talk to the other athletes and get you the jock vote?"

Bryce nods and smiles. "I hope so," he says. "Though the pod is probably quiet right now because of your mural. So I should really be thanking you."

I shrug, feeling my cheeks heat, so I stand up and grab my laptop. I put on *Train to Busan*, just for background noise and to change the subject. It works. Bryce asks me why I like horror movies and books so much, and I'm grateful.

"I think I started watching them because they made the bad things in my life seem less scary," I reveal to him. "Remember how I told you guys I was sick a lot as a kid?" Bryce nods. "Well, yeah. It could be pretty scary at times. So I think reading about haunted hotels and watching serial killers go on rampages just put surgery into perspective. It was like, yeah, I have to spend the night in the hospital, but at least a creepy little girl isn't climbing out of the TV."

"Which reminds me, what do you think of a button with a zombie hand holding dice?"

By the end of the night we have finalized designs for stickers, pins, and one brand-new poster idea—one aimed directly at jocks that we're excited to show our other friends. I shoot a picture of it to Zay for his feedback, and he immediately replies with lots of laughing emojis and a thumbs-up.

We show my mom and Romy our work too, and they think it all looks great. Romy compliments my drawing and Mom says, "I'm so glad Jordyn met you, Bryce. You and your friends seem like a really great influence on her."

I feel something weird in the pit of my gut when she says that, like she doesn't think I can make good choices on my own, but Bryce ducks his head and blushes at her compliment. I'm glad it makes him feel good.

As I walk him out to his car, Bryce clears his throat so I know he's about to speak. "I wish my parents were impressed with anything I do," he says. "You're lucky you have that. It's hard when no one sees you even when you're doing everything you can to make them proud."

I know my parents are supportive of my art, and I worry if I tell Bryce I know what he means, he won't believe me. But if the last two years have shown me anything, it's that I still have a lot to prove before my parents see me the way they once did. All I say is "Bryce, trust me. We have way more in common than you think."

By Sunday some of the interviews from last week start making the rounds online. They had gone live the same day all the press had been in front of Edgewood, but as the news about Zay being clean spreads, people start posting about it using the hashtag, and links to that morning's interviews pop back up too, especially any clips that mentioned him by name. The group chat explodes again since everyone is excited and happy for Zay, and we all make fun of Anton's interview when it resurfaces, because his hair is blowing across his face in a way that makes him continually shake his head to get the strands away from his eyes. Bryce calls him Anton Bieber, and Kaleb takes the most unflattering screenshots he can capture, making us all crack up.

During dinner, I giggle every time I look down at my phone. After the fourth or fifth time, Daddy says, "Okay, Jordyn. No more phone until we're done eating." He takes it away from me and settles it on the mantel. We can still hear it vibrating from the dinner table, so I rush through the rest of the meal, worried I'm missing out.

As soon as I retrieve my phone from the mantel and head to my room, I see that I have a bunch of missed calls from Anton. Just as I'm about to call him back, worried that maybe all the teasing has gotten to him, my phone rings again. I pick up.

"Hey," I say, sounding apprehensive despite myself. "You okay?"

"Hey," he says. "So, look, New Girl. Don't be mad."

"Oh God, Anton, what did you do?" I ask as my heartbeat picks up speed.

"With all the attention on the mural, I thought it would look weird if I didn't post a photo of it since I'm always posting photos from school and around the neighborhood, you, know?"

"I could see that," I admit, still nervous about what he might be about to say.

"So I took this really cool shot yesterday after school. I waited until the golden hour, you know what that is?"

"Anton, please get to the point," I beg.

"Right, well, long story short, I took a great photo with Frida. Gave it a quick-and-dirty edit, and posted it last night. It got a bunch of likes and comments, and I didn't expect anything else to happen. But this art publication reached out to me about a half hour ago and said they wanted to feature my photo in the article they're doing about the mural and asked if I had any other photos they could use for the piece. They said they thought having a student perspective and featuring photographs taken by a student would give their article a leg up in addition to the angle they want for the article: 'art as activism.' I think they saw my interview, the one that you all think is soooo funny, and wanted to hear more from me."

I let out a sigh of relief and immediately think about the zine I need to work on for Roderick's class. The article is exactly on theme, and I can probably pull from the interview for some of the content. "That's great, Anton! Why would that make me mad? This is amazing exposure for you and your photography. And it could help me with a project I need to do for Digital Design."

He's quiet for a beat before he says, "So that's the thing. I kind of got excited when I was talking to them and accidentally mentioned that I knew who had painted the mural."

"Oh," I say. And for a long time, I don't say anything else.

"I didn't tell them it was you!" he rushes to add. "I just blurted out that the person who did it was someone whose art I really admire before I realized what I was saying, but they latched onto it quick. They said they'd like to interview that person too—that this could be another way to differentiate their coverage. If I could offer them an exclusive, it would really give my photo a big moment because other publications would want to pick it up and run it too. And they're willing to pay us."

"Really?" I ask. They must want this interview badly, then.

"Yeah. They were already planning to pay me for my photo, which I think is so cool. You can tell they really believe creating art is work. But it could be fun, and a little bit of a power play, right? Coming forward for a tiny indie art mag instead of the big news organizations that have been chasing answers all week. They could hide your name or face, disguise your voice, anything you'd want if you'd consider doing the interview. I think it would be worth it," Anton says.

I swallow hard, unsure of what to say. I don't know how upset

Anton might be if I say no. And I had hoped to linger in this space of calm for a bit longer. I still don't want to risk being caught. "I don't know," I say.

"I know it's a big favor to ask," Anton says. "But think about it, okay?"

13

# 13

I think about Anton's proposal all night, and when I wake up, I'm still so unsure about what I should do.

"I just wish Anton hadn't said anything," I whisper to Kaleb in first period. I scribble down Roderick's homework assignment and slam my notebook shut. "Things were finally calming down, finally going well. Zay's out of trouble, and it looks like Bryce could actually win this election. I was hoping for the opportunity to lay low for a while, relax a bit and enjoy junior year. Anton had to go and ruin it."

Kaleb gives me the side-eye. "Why are you so upset? It's not like you to be this dramatic, and this is Anton we're talking about. Sweet, silly, goofy Anton. He'd never do anything to make you mad on purpose, and didn't he give you an out?"

I throw my backpack over my shoulder and roll my eyes. "Yeah, I guess," I mumble.

"What's really going on?" Kaleb asks.

"I think all the attention on the mural has just been stressful," I say. "And when Roderick used the word *vandalism*, it made me nervous. I *cannot* afford to get in trouble with my parents again, after everything that happened last year," I add, which is much more than I planned on saying.

Kaleb nods. "I get that," he says. "So don't do it. Tell Anton you don't want to."

I nod like I agree and it's all settled, but the truth is there's something else racing through my brain like a high-speed train: The right thing to do is to be honest, to own up to what I've done, to take responsibility and to help Anton no matter what. And if I'm a good person, a *different* person than I was before, shouldn't I do that without hesitation?

I skip the cafeteria, worried my bad mood will ruin everyone else's lunch break, and head to the library. Part of me thinks sitting somewhere quiet and sketching will help me clear my head and decide what I should do about the interview. But also, I know Zay sometimes does his homework in the stacks during the break, and I wouldn't mind seeing him.

The library is bright and quiet when I walk in, carrying my backpack on one arm and holding my sketchbook, already open to a new page, in the other. The stacks are high, but plenty of sunshine still spills through the towering shelves, and dust motes float like lazy gnats in every ray of light. I post up at a table by a big window and begin filling the page in front of me with tall trees, branches sprouting away from the trunks like thin and wild networks of veins. The trees remind me of lies, how they can take root and grow bigger than you'd ever planned, reaching unexpected people and places, and just as I begin to add unruly grasses and a murky pond that I imagine as being filled with secrets, I feel more than hear someone behind me.

"Hey," Zay says, just before his warm hand lands on my shoulder. "Isn't lunch like prime gossip time for you and Mila? What are you doing in here?"

I look up at him, and see that he's studying my sketchbook, the dark forest I've drawn, the way my fingers are smudged with graphite. "You good?" he asks, and I shake my head, tears pricking behind my eyes.

"Hey, hey," Zay says softly, concern crowding his features. He slides into the chair beside me and moves it closer to mine. "What's going on?"

"Some artsy site wants to publish one of Anton's photos of the mural and write a piece on it," I pout.

Zay nods, but I can tell he's confused. "Shouldn't that be a good thing?"

"It is. But Anton mentioned that he knew who painted it, so now they also want to interview that person. Me."

"Ah," Zay says. "And you don't want to get in trouble."

I nod, thinking about Bryce saying how hard it is when you want to make your parents proud but nothing you do feels good enough. "Anton said they'd use a fake name, but I'm still scared. I don't know what will happen."

Zay's quiet for a moment, and I can tell he's measuring his words carefully, deciding what the right thing is to say. He leans forward and whispers, "I think you should do it."

"What?" I ask. "Why?"

Wordlessly, Zay takes out his phone, pulls up his email, and hands it to me. His inbox is packed with messages, and most look to be from universities, news companies, and nonprofit organizations. I look back up at him, my eyes full of questions.

"Ever since *my* interview after the team's drug tests all came back clean, the attention has been constant. Other places want to interview me, schools I hadn't even applied to are reaching out, and a bunch of organizations I've never heard of are offering me scholarships."

I feel my eyes widen.

"Now, I understand why you wouldn't want to reveal yourself. And it could definitely have consequences that we're not thinking about right now. But I think it could also be a huge opportunity. I mean, you told me how badly you want to go to art school. Think about how cool it could be to have an article about you in an art magazine before you graduate? Think about how you could add the mural to your portfolio and how much this kind of work could make you stand out on your applications. Hell, you could even use it as the subject of one of your college essays."

He's right. I can't imagine my parents being too upset about it if I did it for the right reasons, *and* it helped me get into college. "Wow. I hadn't considered any of that," I say.

He stands up, kisses my forehead, and tugs on my ear, as if his work here is done. "Now you have," he says. "I gotta go finish some stuff up since I have practice this afternoon, but if you wanna talk about this more, call me tonight."

I smile up at him, tug his belt loop to pull him closer, and he gets the message. He leans down and I stretch up until our lips meet. "Thanks, Zay," I tell him.

"Anytime," he whispers.

I sit there with my drawing for the rest of the lunch period, thinking about what Zay said, and lots of other things too. I'm tired of keeping secrets, of hiding, of choosing my actions based purely on surviving. And frankly, it's exhausting. If I'm really different than I was before, I'll need to move differently all the time, not just when it's safe. And the only reason any of this is still scary to me is because I'm letting everyone else hold the power I've been working for weeks to take away from the podcaster. I decide who I am, how I move, what I do. Refusing to own up to the things I've done is what got me here in the first place. It's time I stop operating from a place of fear and practice what I've been preaching.

Right before I get up to leave, I add a girl to the edge of the forest in my drawing. It looks like she's been lost in the dark for a long time and she's finally stepping into the light.

---

The next afternoon is the big student assembly where everyone running for student government will deliver their speeches. Kaleb, Anton, Mila, and I spend all morning handing out the buttons and stickers I designed for Bryce, and most of lunch posting his campaign images all over our online profiles and pages as one final hurrah. Bryce is a bundle of nerves all day, and we reassure him in every way we can that he's done a great job campaigning. By the time we all file into the auditorium and take our seats, I think we all feel we've done everything in our power to support him.

The secretaries and treasurers speak first, and by the time the vice presidential candidates make their speeches, I'm practically vibrating with excitement. Peyton speaks before Bryce does, which I hope will work in his favor. Her speech is delivered mostly in concrete terms about the changes she could make, the impact she could have on very specific aspects of the way Edgewood functions: how events are organized and the ways money is raised—who has power and how that power can be redistributed more fairly. She gets a standing ovation when she's done speaking, so when it's Bryce's turn, we all stand and scream at the top of our lungs before he even begins his speech. He speaks in terms of the abstract: He imagines a better future for the school that gives space to everyone's voice; he pitches a complete shift in the culture of gossip and bullying; he talks about how students and teachers could work together more if only they tried. He ends strong with his *Don't roll the dice, vote for Bryce!* slogan, and we stand and scream again for him until he beams with pride.

As we line up to cast our votes, I turn over both Peyton's and Bryce's speeches in my head. He told a great story, but Peyton explained exactly how she'd make her goals a reality, and I worry the results will come down to this: Kids who want results, and kids who want hope. I hope that if I do the interview with Anton, I can offer both.

———————

"What makes a person good? What makes a person bad? How do you know which kind of person you are or which kind you're becoming?" I hear myself say. "Too often I think our opinions of who someone is, of who we are ourselves, are based on what other people say."

I'm on a video call with a woman named Valentina from *State of the Arts*, the media site that wants to write about the mural. She has long, straight dark hair, wide, white-framed glasses, and serious eyes that don't move from my face as I speak. Anton is here too, in a second, smallish square on my screen. She started the interview with him, and now it's my turn. He's smiling, while Valentina nods seriously, and I continue trying to answer her question about how we decided that a public act like this one would be the right way to address the abusive nature of the podcast.

"For me, the mural was about giving people a chance to speak their truth before it was spoken for them. It was about putting power back into the rightful owners' hands. And you can't do something like that quietly. The podcast stole stories and broadcast them without permission—without input from the person the story belonged to. I wanted the podcaster to know that was wrong, and to give people a chance to reveal their secrets—or not—but in their own words, and in their own time.

Valentina nods and I hear her typing, taking notes, even though I know the call is being recorded too. I decided not to hide, gave her my real name, and I'm using my real voice. Clips from this call may appear on their website and I'll be quoted in a written piece they're doing too.

"And is Tomcat Tea over?" she asks me next. "Did you achieve what you set out to do?"

"I can't say for sure that the podcast is over for good, but I think we did what we wanted: Kids at our school, and people in other places too, are telling their own stories, owning up to things they've done, things that may have brought them shame. But they're saying 'That's not all I am,' or even just 'That's not who I am anymore.' I think there's power in that."

"And is that enough for you? Or are you hoping this mural has a longer tail? A lasting impact?" Valentina asks.

I'm reminded of Bryce's speech—the way he pitched a better school, a better world. The way he told a story that had a foundation of hope.

"I think it's a natural human inclination to want to make bad things better. To want to help. And the desire to help comes from a belief that you can. That individual people have the power to make a difference." Images of Bree fill my head, of all the times I watched her cry, convinced I couldn't do anything about it. "I spent a lot of time feeling powerless—feeling like nothing I did or could do would matter. So I think the most important thing this mural has done is made me realize that isn't true. It's made me see in real time that I can make a difference, that the choices I make matter. That my actions are louder than words. I feel proud that if nothing else, it's done that."

Valentina nods and asks a few more questions of me and Anton before telling us the story will go live the following week. She signs off, and Anton video calls me back as soon as she ends the meeting.

"You were amazing!" he says.

I laugh a little and shrug. "So were you."

"Do you really believe all that stuff you said?" he asks me.

I think about the power of storytelling—all the ways it can harm; all the ways it can help. I think about the stories I've told myself about the people around me, and about myself. I think, in the same way I want to speak for myself, I want everyone else to have that opportunity too.

This feels like too much to put into words. So, to Anton, all I say is "Yep."

---

It doesn't take a week. A few days later, Bryce gets a notification from his search alerts that *State of the Arts* has posted a video. It's a clip from our interview, and there's my face, big and undeniable, saying that I painted the mural. I immediately start to sweat, tension making my shoulders inch closer to my ears, because, when I made this, it felt theoretical, not real, that I'd revealed myself as the mural's artist, until this very moment.

Kaleb, Mila, and Bryce are ecstatic, but my heart is pounding. Part of me regrets coming forward, and I immediately want to run and hide. To calm myself down, I try to breathe deeply, and draw a self-portrait in my mind. I make the mental-sketch-version of myself into a superhero, standing on a rooftop in a dark and gothic comic book version of Washington, DC.

I summon every bit of courage I have left, even as I continue to add graffiti to the city walls I'm building around the hero version of myself in my head. I send the link to Zay, unsure how long it will be before it's found by anyone else, but praying the reveal is slow and easy. I'm still terrified of what the consequences could be at school—what my parents might do or say. But for now it feels like a victory, watching myself speak truths in real time, seeing the messages of support from my friends.

I go to bed feeling a little calmer, my heart and belly a bit warm and fuzzy because of how proud my friends and Zay seem to be of me. I begin to feel proud of myself too once I'm calmer, good in the way I've always wanted to be—like I've done something right for once.

I cue up the video one more time to watch Anton talking about technique and how all kinds of art can make a difference—how historically it has been a part of so many movements. When my face appears on the screen again, I check the views, and they're steadily ticking upward, already in the thousands, and my phone vibrates next to me on the bed. I grab my phone as the interview ends, flick through messages from the group chat and a few from Zay. Until a new message appears.

A text from the private number pops up almost as soon as the interview finishes playing and restarts again on my laptop screen.

*Jordyn, Jordyn, Jordyn . . .* it reads.

*I warned you not to be a hero.*

# HARTWELL ACADEMY
# UPPER SCHOOL ATHLETICS FIELD
# 4 MONTHS AGO

I've always hated gym. I'm an artsy girl, not an athletic one—always have been. So when I got a devastating cramp in my side while trying to complete the mile run we had to do every semester, I wasn't surprised.

It was May, and the sun was finally shining after nearly a week of rain, so our class was on the outdoor track surrounding the muddy field where the cheerleaders and soccer girls usually practiced. "Coach Yardley?" I called as I doubled over, panting. "Can I take a breather?"

"Come on, Jordyn," Lilly called. "You got this!" She and Yasmine were neck and neck, running as fast as their designer sneakers could carry them. And Elise was already done, her access to a personal trainer and home gym showing more than she would ever admit.

"No breathers, Jones," Coach Yardley shouted. "Unless you want an incomplete."

I looked around at which girls were stragglers like I was, struggling their way to the finish line. I did it mostly out of self-preservation—I was sure if I didn't finish before girls like Jamie Donovan or Olive White, who were teased because of their weight and large breasts, respectively, I'd never live it down. But as I scanned the track, I noticed, maybe for the first time that class period, that Aubrey wasn't there.

As I limped around the track, easing into my final lap, I realized that I hadn't seen Aubrey all day. Had she been cleaning her glasses in the chem lab or cowering next to her locker in the hall? I couldn't remember. I'd missed her at lunch too, didn't see her sitting by herself in the corner at the table closest to the exit. It was only weird because Aubrey never missed school—she'd always prided herself on perfect attendance, even when we were in middle school.

When I caught up with Ruby Chan, Aubrey's lab partner and a sweet girl who was kind to everyone, I wheezed out, "You seen Aubrey today?"

Ruby shook her head. "I texted her too because we had this big project due today. Super weird but looks like she ghosted."

Before I could process how unlike Aubrey it was to miss school, especially on the due date of an important assignment, I saw Vice Principal Valentine and Dean Murphy walk out onto the track. The vice principal crossed her arms and Dean Murphy beckoned Elise to come over to where they were standing. I stopped running.

"Yeah, Daddy?" I heard Elise say. I couldn't make out the dean's reply, but I didn't need to. Elise's face paled, her mouth dropping open, her eyes widening in disbelief. I watched as Vice Principal Valentine asked Coach Yardley a question, and then through the same megaphone the gym teacher had been using to bark commands at the students as we ran around the track, she cleared her throat and said, "I need Yasmine Thorne, Lilliana Sandoval, and Jordyn Jones over here, please. You can finish your miles another day. The rest of you, keep running."

I looked around for Yasmine and Lilly, and found them slowing down, breathing hard, turning to look in the direction of Coach Yardley's voice. I started toward the three adults and Elise, something in my belly pulling tight as a knot.

"What's going on?" Lilly asked as soon as we were all standing together. Yasmine bent forward, fixing her ponytail. I had both hands on my hips, trying to slow my breathing, and my heart was squeezing in a way that made my chest ache.

"We need you to answer a few questions. It's about a student.

Aubrey Day," Dean Murphy said. He looked at his daughter as if he was telling her not to speak, even as he told us he had questions. Elise still looked terrified. I rubbed my sweaty palms down the front of my shorts, knowing the clamminess wasn't only from running.

"What about her?" Yasmine asked. She sounded genteel. Clueless. Innocent. But I could see what was coming. That something had happened, and it made my heart speed up. I knew that we were already or soon would be in trouble.

"I think we should do this in my office," Vice Principal Valentine suggested. "More privacy."

I nodded. Yasmine shrugged. Lilly said, "Okay."

But Elise said, "Oh my God, it isn't our fault that girl hates herself."

Me, Yasmine, and Lilly all frowned in Elise's direction, confused. "What?" I said.

"If anything," Elise continued, like someone possessed, "it's Jordyn's fault. She's the one who was friends with her and then totally turned on her when she came here. She's the reason Aubrey even expected to have friends at Hartwell."

I felt the heat in my body rising. I still didn't know what was happening, just that Elise was hanging me out to dry, throwing me under the bus, blaming me for something I didn't even fully understand yet. I felt something darken in me, like a cloud had come and covered whatever light I'd been holding inside.

"You're the one who tortured her, almost on the daily," I shot back. "Lilly and Yasmine were with you too, doing the most, being the worst. Don't even try to act like you're innocent in this. Whatever this is."

"Girls. My office, please," Vice Principal Valentine said, but teenage girls are hard to control once activated, and I could feel every bit of anger I'd pushed down all year rearing up in me like tiny, individual fires. I was a constellation of candles, flames flickering in the dark. If one fell, it would set everything around it alight.

"Oh please," Elise said, ignoring Mrs. Valentine. I thought maybe she felt untouchable with Dean Daddy so close; maybe she thought she could do or say whatever she wanted to save herself without repercussions. "You were a part of it too. If anything, you gave us more ammo. If anything, you were the reason we even noticed her."

I stepped closer to Elise, feeling the weight of months of silence settle on my shoulders. I knew Elise had a point, but I couldn't stomach it, couldn't handle the guilt of what my silence might have cost.

*Where was Aubrey?*

"Shut up," I said. And Elise laughed. "I said, shut the hell up."

Elise rolled her eyes and something inside me cracked open.

I stepped even closer to Elise, and when Elise stepped back, she tripped and tumbled into a mud puddle. Elise screamed and said, "Oh my God, why are you *attacking* me? Daddy, she's attacking me!"

I looked at Dean Murphy—at Elise's father—as he stooped to pick his daughter up by the elbow. "Watch yourself, Jordyn," he said, his tone low and threatening. "This is already a very complicated situation. You don't want to look worse than you already do." His voice and his posture were a warning.

But I wasn't afraid anymore, at least not of them. Something was very wrong. I could feel it.

I couldn't help but think about the day Aubrey and I met. We'd been fifth graders, starting at a middle school that was full of kids much bigger than we were. Aubrey had been wearing a huge novelty T-shirt with the original *Texas Chainsaw Massacre* movie art on it, and my favorite movie was *Halloween*, so I'd walked over to her right away and asked her who she thought was scarier, Leatherface or Michael Myers.

"Oh, Michael Myers for sure. Leatherface only killed you if you came to him. Michael went after people." Her answer had made my day. We kept talking, and soon discovered we'd both been born too early, that we'd both been sick a lot as little kids. We were both too familiar with the potently clean scent of hospitals, the prick of needles and papery crinkle of exam tables, the icy chill of IV fluid slipping into our veins. We were small and scarred because we'd survived something—and we were still surviving. It was why we loved scary movies—we liked to imagine we would always be the last ones standing.

In addition to horror movies, we both loved thrifting and making weird keepsakes out of things we found, Stephen King novels, and blasting hip-hop so loud the floors of our bedrooms vibrated with bass. Our friendship had been birthed from our many commonalities, but it was then forged in fire—when we were teased about our clothes or our size or our strangeness, we cried together, or fought back together, or made a plan to exact revenge together. We'd promised to be together forever.

But then Aubrey had gotten into that boarding school—had received a full ride. And though Bree tried to explain to me why she had to go, I didn't listen. I just heard that my best friend was leaving, that I'd have to start all over, that once again I'd have to face the world alone.

I had gone to Hartwell with one goal: to survive. If middle school had taught me anything, it was that the truest version of who I was was too weird to make sense to most people. I couldn't risk being rejected without a friend I could trust to love the real me. So I needed a persona. A Jordyn I could perform who always said the right thing and who liked normal stuff and who got along with everyone. I just had to survive high school, and then there would be college. Hopefully art school, where I'd be surrounded by people who didn't fit into boxes—people like the real me. So I straightened my hair. I hid anything that made me too different. I found the most powerful girls in school and made them into allies.

Even though I wasn't exactly happy, I was safe. I was surviving. So my plan had worked, was working, until Bree called to say she hated the boarding school, to say she was transferring to Hartwell. And I didn't know how to make my old friend fit into my new life; I didn't know how to be around someone who knew the version of myself I'd buried.

Finally, I said, "Where is Aubrey?"

Without blinking, the dean answered. "There's been an accident."

Elise chewed her bottom lip. Yasmine and Lilly looked at each other. I was shaking because I knew "accident" was a euphemism for something much darker.

"My office," Mrs. Valentine said. *"Now."*

Well, well, well . . . I'm back. Did you miss me? A weeklong hiatus was needed, and thanks to the wonderful "artist" who painted that tacky mural—you've made my job way easier. Thanks for hand delivering me the tea. I'm wondering who you could be just as much as you're wondering the same thing about me. This is gonna be a fun game to play! Now, let's get into our weekly recap.

For drama, Peyton actually did indeed land the lead part in *Into the Woods* and her male lead will be played by Joshua Brooks. Break a leg Peyton, Joshua, and the rest of the cast. To all those who didn't get a part, well, better luck next time!

When it comes to the student government campaign, the stakes have been raised. According to an insider, Bryce and Peyton are neck and neck. They've been campaigning all over school, and I've even heard rumors that the teachers are running a betting pool over the outcome. One thing's for sure, those two have genuinely shown the true definition of competitiveness, and the race can go either way.

Let's get into the tea, shall we? Troy Perry got a weeklong

suspension this week for starting a fire in the bathroom. His defense was that he was just trying to smoke (which . . . doesn't exactly help his case) and a toilet paper roll caught on fire. And in trying to put it out, he inadvertently unwound the roll, just spreading the fire even more. Yeah . . . okay. Bye, Troy!

Now, for our BOMBSHELL. This is serious news, but I have a duty to report the truth. Before we get into it, I want to give a trigger warning: The information I am about to share includes mentions of bullying and attempted suicide. Out of respect for the survivor, we are choosing to keep the name of the innocent party anonymous.

It seems like supposed do-gooder Jordyn has truly been hiding a dark secret. We've gotten to the bottom of why she's here. Apparently at her old school, she and her friends tortured a fellow student until she eventually attempted, but thankfully survived, a suicide attempt. I've learned the girl and Jordyn used to be close friends . . . until Jordyn changed. Jordyn changed her hair, her clothes, and even her attitude just to fit in, and she left her bestie behind. I guess she thought having her five seconds of high school fame would be worth the expense of another girl's mental health. Watch out for Jordyn—seems like she can reinvent herself all she wants, but in the end she's really just a terrible mean girl and a bully. I'm sorry to have to report this, but Edgewood deserves to know.

Who are the people we really go to school with? Who are they behind closed doors? In the case of Jordyn Jones, we finally know the truth.

# JORDYN'S DMS

**Podthrill_76:**

Hypocrite.

**xxmessyjessixx:**

Liar.

**AnnaKDuval:**

You drove someone to attempt suicide and now you're acting like you're so good?

**Misschocolate216:**

fake ass

**rugbeerizz:**

WOW

**Thisisryanstine:**

How you gonna make a movement called #nomoresecrets and still be keeping one as big as this??

**Whisper2crush:**

Seems a little convenient. Owning up to the mural, then getting your spot blown up on the pod . . .

**CardiCee:**

huge bully pretending to be everybody's friend? i cannot.

**Naaaaaandi:**

lolllllllllll

**unalexis:**

You prolly didn't even paint the mural!

**Yourexlover5:**

Omg, this you?

🔗 STATE OF THE ARTS

## Art as Activism:
*How a Mural by Student Jordyn Jones Changed the Culture at Edgewood High*

**Poeticaaas:**

I don't believe a word you say.

**Animaltracxxs:**

jesus. bffr.

**Vanvan99:**

Is "Jordyn" even your real name?

**Asherwoods:**

Had EVERYBODY fooled

**Margauxgo:**

Phony.

**Lemonnadia:**

I knew you were sus from the start.

# 14

When I wake up, my DMs are overflowing with messages, but the group chat is oddly silent except a single message from Bryce: *Is it true?* I don't want to lie, but I don't want to say yes either. Everyone at Edgewood thinks I'm a fraud, and I know all too well the weight and pain of the loneliness that could be coming my way if my friends agree.

The momentary joy I felt from speaking up about the mural has disappeared. I also think some part of me knew that the podcaster would be back, but I ignored the feeling, opting instead to believe in the tentative, temporary peace. I silence my notifications, get dressed quickly, and send a pleading message to the group chat. *When everyone gets to school, can we please talk?*

No one answers as I eat a quick breakfast, lace up my boots, and slip on my coat, or while I'm standing at the bus stop. I wonder if my nonanswer is answer enough for them. I start to get antsy once I board the bus and I'm on my way to school, and when I get there and there's still no text back, I don't know what I'm walking into. I just want a chance for them to hear my side of the story. I'm terrified they won't listen.

The hallways feel just as they did on the first day: wide and wild, lonely and loud. I swing by Kaleb's locker, but he isn't there. I look for Mila and Anton, but I don't see either of them in the long corridors where they usually linger before class. I do find Bryce, talking to Peyton in the senior hall, but when I start toward him, he shakes his head and moves quickly down the hall away from me.

"Bryce, wait!" I shout, but he keeps walking like he can't hear the sound of my voice. He turns a corner and is gone before I can reach him.

It's then that I feel the eyes. Everyone is looking at me, but this feels very different from the first day of school. When I first got to Edgewood, the looks were cautious but curious. But now some of the students are giggling, some are sneering, and others just shake their heads. They all have judgment in their eyes, and they all angle their bodies away from me. Without deciding to, my mind wanders to Bree and I wonder if this is how she felt at Hartwell.

In Roderick's class, Kaleb doesn't look my way for the entire period, and when I catch his arm while he's packing up his stuff to head out, he sighs and turns toward me. "I just want to talk," I say, my voice sounding more desperate than I want it to.

"I know. But when Bryce asked you if it was true, you didn't deny it. So before we talk, just tell me: Did you and your friends really bully a girl until she wanted to die?"

His question lands like a hammer. His hazel eyes are steady and waiting. Because he phrased it in precisely that way, I can't say no, or that it didn't happen. "Kaleb, please," I whine, my voice already thick with tears. He grabs his things and leaves without looking back at me.

When I bump into Mila in the hallway between classes, she gives me the cold shoulder too, and I wonder if Kaleb has already told her what he asked me. How I couldn't say no. I start with saying, "I can explain," and she frowns and blinks at me like I'm speaking a language she doesn't understand. "How could you possibly explain standing by while your friend is tortured? Would you even say anything if people were coming for me?"

"Of course I would," I say, "and things with Bree were . . . complicated."

Mila scoffs. "Yeah, okay," she says before she walks away without another word.

It isn't until I find Anton right before lunch that the reality of what it will be like to lose all my friends at once sinks in. Anton's usually all bright-eyed and full of jokes. But when he sees me, his naturally warm expression falls. I see him swallow hard, but he doesn't walk away as I approach. And when I reach him, all he says is "Damn, New Girl. How does something like that even happen?"

He waits, like he really wants to hear me out. But everyone else's reaction has taught me that what I have to say doesn't matter. My past actions are so much louder than any of my words in this moment. Nothing I say will change the fact that they all see that I'm a monster now. I shrug. "I don't know," I say to Anton, and I wonder if he can tell how close I feel to crying. I'm worried if I share too much right here, I'll lose it. And I can't afford to cry right now.

At lunchtime I avoid the cafeteria because I can't handle more stares, and I know I wouldn't be welcome at my regular table. But I do send a message to the group chat telling them I'm ready to talk when they're ready to listen. *I don't want to make excuses but if it matters*, I add, *I really have tried my best to change. After last year, I vowed to never be a bystander again. And I've kept that promise.*

I head to the library again, looking for Zay. I don't know if he'll believe me, but under the library's high ceilings, between the quiet, close shelves, I feel like I might find the words to explain. I dip my head into the stacks, checking them row by row until I find him sitting at the corner of a table, a notebook open in front of him, his head hovering so close to the page that I know he's drawing.

"Hey," I say softly. He looks up, and his eyes darken a little, but he sits back and nods at the chair across from him. I read it as an invitation. I pull out the chair, slip my bag from my shoulder, and sink down before letting out a choked sigh.

"You okay?" Zay asks, not unkindly. But his normal softness is nowhere to be found.

I nod, then shake my head. Laugh a little darkly. "Not really," I answer honestly.

"You wanna talk about it?" he asks, and I do, but I need to know something first.

"Will you believe me if I tell you the truth?"

Zay looks thoughtful, and I like that he doesn't answer right away. Because of his hesitation, I can tell that when he does, what he says is true.

"I'm pissed that the podcast is back. I'm pissed that they came for you after you put yourself out there. And I'm pissed that you hid something this big. But yeah. I'll believe you, the same way you listened when I told you about Peyton. Besides, at this point, there's no reason for you to hide."

Just before I begin to speak, a crackle fills the air around us, the office intercom coming to life. "The election results are in: Peyton Reynolds is your new student body president. We congratulate all the candidates on their excellent campaign efforts and look forward to a year of great improvement here at Edgewood High."

My eyes fill, but the tears don't fall, though my throat throbs. Failing Bryce compounds my feelings of guilt. But I clear my throat, glance down at Zay's notebook where he'd been drawing a pair of hands cradling a bird, and desperately hope that that's how he'll hold my truth.

I try to speak, but fear chokes me, holding my voice hostage. "Can I tell you tomorrow?" I whisper, needing a little more time to prepare myself to reveal the secret.

"Of course," he says. "Take all the time you need. Sit down. Today, let's just draw."

We sit in the quiet together, only the sounds of pencils scratching paper keeping us company, and I pray that once he knows the truth, I won't lose him too.

# OASIS IN THE WOODS
# PRIVATE OUTDOOR POOL
# 2 MONTHS AGO

I had begged to cancel the party.

When my parents and I made the plan to have a huge birthday pool party featuring an exclusive, secluded resort and a well-loved local radio personality as the DJ, things at school had been very different. By the time everything went sideways, it was too late for them to cancel without losing thousands of dollars. Plus, they felt I deserved a bit of a celebration for surviving the drama and still completing my credits remotely in spite of everything.

I straightened the strap of my new fuchsia bikini and walked the full perimeter of the pool again, trying to calm my breathing. The inflatable flamingo floats and beach balls looked like something out of a magazine atop the clear blue of the water, and the paper lanterns strung above alternated in a hot pink and cheerful orange, perfectly matching my suit and the rest of the décor.

It was the kind of Sweet Sixteen I'd dreamed of without the hope it would ever come true. But it was happening, it was real. The only problem? I was still the only one there.

I hadn't had the heart to tell my family what I already knew—the party was destined to be a disaster. To tell them how ugly things had gotten the day I'd found out what had really happened to Bree. How Lilly and Yasmine had taken Elise's side, how my "friends" had told the entire school that everything that had happened with Bree had been all my fault, and that I was mean, violent, even "psycho." How I'd been shunned from group chats and unfriended and blocked. That even after I'd done horrible things all in the hope to make and keep friends, it hadn't saved me.

"Where is everyone?" Mom asked no one in particular for the third or fourth time. I tried not to think about Daddy, who was across the resort, in the Oasis kitchen with a few of his Bread & Butter sous chefs, making the lunch platters that, because of me, would rot and go to waste.

"I think I'll go double-check with the front desk that no one needs the gate code," Mom said, nervously twisting her rings while heading inside.

"Should we call anyone?" Romy asked, coming to sit beside me as I finally stopped pacing. I shook my head. But when Romy put her warm hand on my shoulder, it unlocked something feral inside me. The gentleness of my aunt's touch untied whatever up until that point had been holding me together.

"No one is going to come, Romy. And I knew this would happen." I started sobbing, the tears pouring from my eyes, my breathing coming too fast in too-short bursts, and Romy had to hold both my hands and tell me to put my head between my knees to stop me from hyperventilating. "So, you know how I told you they expelled me because they said I'd attacked Elise, and she's the dean's daughter?" I asked. Romy nodded. "Well, that wasn't the whole story."

Romy sat up straighter. She frowned. "So what really happened?"

"When we found out that Bree had made the . . . attempt . . . it was chaos. We were all crowded into Principal Valentine's office, just standing there, and Dean Murphy just said it so casually. He's like, 'Aubrey Day was found unconscious in her room last night. She'd taken an entire bottle of her mother's painkillers. She'd written a note.' They didn't tell us exactly what it said—but I guess her mom had found our names somewhere, in the note or her journal or something, and that's why we were in trouble."

"Oh my God," Romy said.

"Yeah. Elise just loses it, starts crying so hard saying it's all made up and that Bree is lying because she's jealous of her. Elise was saying all this stuff about how Bree was dramatic, and that she'd never done anything to her. How she couldn't help it if she was popular and had good grades and it wasn't her fault that no one liked Bree. And I just couldn't deal anymore, you know? We'd been so shitty to Bree for so long, and I wasn't about to let Elise wiggle her way out of it." I had to stop talking for a second because I started crying again. I pulled my feet out of the pool and hugged my legs to my chest, imagining Bree feeling that alone and hopeless.

"So I said, 'The only person lying right now is you, Elise. A girl almost died. How can you be so heartless?' She didn't like that."

"I bet," Romy said, crossing her arms.

"That's when Elise came for me. She said I'd acted alone. That I was the one who had been friends with Bree before, so wouldn't it make sense if we had a friend breakup and hated each other now? That maybe that's why our names were in her note or journal or whatever—Aubrey hated me because I'd forgotten about her and wanted to take down the friends who had stolen me from her too."

"Oh no," Romy said. "That makes a little too much sense."

"Right? I got scared. I thought they'd believe her over me. And Yasmine and Lilly were ready to go along with it—I could tell. So

I grabbed her wrist, just to get her to turn around and see that I wasn't going to let her get away with lying. But as soon as I touched her, she flipped out, shook me off, and pushed me, hard. And I fell backward into the door. The handle dug into my back, and it hurt like hell. When I recovered, I punched her right in the face. Gave her a black eye. *That's* why I got expelled, even though she pushed me first. They claimed me touching her wrist was the first 'blow.'

"But I'm pretty sure that after that, Elise, Lilly, and Yasmine told everyone that I'd attacked Elise. That I was violent and prone to outbursts. And from the looks of things . . . everyone believed them."

Romy pulled me to her. And I cried more, as I would for the rest of the summer whenever I remembered the party, the sinking feeling of being utterly alone, the moment in the principal's office where everything went wrong, or the rumor that I was dangerous.

When I thought about Bree and the part I'd played, there was a part of me that agreed. A part of me felt like I deserved to be alone, if that was how I treated a person I had once loved.

# 15

The next day I meet Zay in the library. We sit at our favorite table by the big windows, and the sunlight turns his dark brown eyes as golden as iced tea. I talk and he listens. I tell him everything my friends didn't let me tell them yesterday.

"Wow, that's a lot," he says. "But . . . and I hope I don't sound like a dick . . . what are you going to do about it?"

"Do about it?" I ask, and I feel a little bit of heat (embarrassment? anger?) creep up my spine. "What do you mean, do about it? I'm trying to be a better person. I've refused to stand silently by all year. I painted the mural. Did that interview . . . ?" I look at him, and I'm sure confusion is all over my face.

"Yeah," he says. "And? What about Bree? Did you ever apologize to her?"

My face burns with shame. My hands shake with the awful truth his question brings to the surface—I thought changing my future behavior would be enough. I say, "There was no time. She disappeared and never came back. I got expelled." But really, I've been too ashamed and angry, with Elise and myself, to seek her out.

"You said you've changed," Zay says softly, continuing to push and challenge me in a way far beyond what I expect. He reaches out for my hand. "But I guess what I'm wondering is: How does that help the person you actually hurt?"

I want to argue with him. To say that *I* wasn't the person who caused the most harm. But before the thought can even fully form in my mind, I stop myself. If I've really changed, why wouldn't I want Bree to know I'm sorry?

I'm surprised by his toughness when Zay is normally so tender. But I realize he's right. Maybe it isn't enough that I've changed. Maybe if I really want to be different, I need to face the person I hurt—do something to really and truly try to make it right, for Bree.

"I'm scared," I admit to Zay. "I lost her, lost all my friends at Hartwell. And now all my friends at Edgewood hate me. What if she doesn't accept my apology?"

"She doesn't have to," Zay says. "It's not about you. Don't you see that?"

His love in that moment feels like Aunt Romy's, hard and soft at the same time. Which makes it feel more real.

"And besides, she might. Just like in soccer when I try to make a goal and I miss? Not to be cheesy," he says, right before he says the cheesiest thing ever, "but you miss one hundred percent of the shots you don't take."

"Oh God," I say, laughing through sudden tears.

He smooths the pads of his thumbs over my cheeks. "You still gotta try," he tells me.

———

The rest of the school day passes in a blur of my friends ignoring me and everyone else throwing dismissive and downright mean looks in my direction. I'm grateful to be seeing Zay again after school, and the second the bell rings, I leave the building as quickly as I can.

When Zay walks into Bread & Butter, he still has beads of water on the nape of his neck from his shower after soccer practice, and I can smell the clean copper scent of him, like a handful of pennies washed with a bar of green soap. He hugs me, and I breathe him in before pushing a plate full of food in his direction.

"I'm starving," he says. "Thank you."

"No, thank *you*," I say.

I sit on the same side of the booth as him, so he can see my phone. Then I search her name.

I hadn't looked at any of Bree's accounts since last year, mostly because I was terrified of what I might find, or worse—to discover that she'd blocked me. But when I click on her profile, photos of her fill my screen. She hasn't blocked me—hasn't even unfollowed me—and something about that makes me feel like there's a tiny, sharp shard of something, lodged and aching, inside my chest.

She looks happy. Her cheeks are rounder and rosier, and her acne scars seem less pronounced. She has new glasses that are a shimmering shade of purple, and she's added a few streaks of blond to her hair. It looks healthier too—shiny and not as weighed down. In every single photo she's smiling, like as her spirit lifted, so did everything else about her, down to the corners of her mouth. Lots of her photos include the hashtag #collegelife, and I realize fairly quickly what must have happened.

"She skipped the rest of high school," I say out loud. "Probably just tested out of eleventh after taking all those AP classes in tenth. And she did twelfth over the summer. She's taking classes at American University. I can't believe it," I say. But then a second later, I realize I can.

"Impressive," Zay says, wiping his hands on a napkin before taking my phone to zoom in on a photo of Bree grinning on a wide green lawn.

"She was always really smart," I tell him. "Like, even in middle school she was in this special program on Saturdays where she got to do all this science stuff in a high school lab. That was how she got a scholarship to the boarding school. And then to Hartwell. It was how we first bonded—us both being so into things other kids thought were weird or boring. It was science and engineering for her, drawing and art for me. And horror movies. We loved them. The bloodier, the better."

I scroll up and down her profile again. "You think it's real?" I ask. "How happy she looks? Do you think she's really doing okay?"

Zay shrugs. "She's still in DC," he says. "You can find out if you really want to. You gonna reach out?"

The thought of it makes my whole body warm, embarrassment and shame flooding my bloodstream like caffeine. "I think so. And as much as I hate to say it, I feel like sending her a DM with an apology would be a bit of a cop-out. She could ignore it, never read it, never reply."

He nods. "She has a right to do that."

"No, I know. It's just that I want her to know I really mean it. I think I want to go by her house. See if she'll talk to me. But I don't know if she even lives in the same place."

On her page I notice other photos of her in front of what look like elementary and middle school students. I wonder if she's become some kind of mentor or something. There's a video too, but I don't watch it here. The hashtag in the caption reads #TheBreeProject, and I save the video to watch it later.

Zay looks thoughtful. "You're sure?" he asks.

"I think so. But there's something else I want to do first."

***

I spend the rest of the night working on sketches of my friends.

I know it's not much, but I spend hours focusing on the details of each of their faces. Anton's eyebrows, like straight black slashes across his forehead, the way his dark eyes always look soft and bright. Kaleb's brown spirals; his long, bristly eyelashes; his mischievous grin. It takes me a solid fifteen minutes to match the golden-brown shade of Mila's skin, to find the perfect way to blend the shadows on her cheek to reveal her dimple. I focus hard on Bryce's blond bangs, curling like a comma over his thin, long face, then on his eyes, green as a traffic light, deep set and serious.

On the back of each portrait, I write a heartfelt apology,

specific to the ways each of them have made me want to grow, to be different, to be better than I was in the past. I tell Kaleb that his willingness to speak up, even against authority, when he sees or hears cruelty makes me want to do the same. Mila's letter details the care she shows for her sisters and her willingness to put herself in harm's way to protect others. I write that her actions make me think and move in less selfish ways. I tell Anton that his kindness and artistic eye help me to think outside the box when it comes to the best ways to make a difference, and in Bryce's letter, I write about how his leadership makes me want to take more action to make school and the world a better place. In all their letters, I explain the truth of what happened with Bree, without making excuses for myself, without blaming anyone else. I end each letter the same way:

*My aunt says that silence is violence, and after last year, I know she's right. It's why I've done everything differently this time around. I hope you can find it in your heart to see and believe that I've changed.*

When I finish, I look at what I've done and worry it's not enough. I think about Bree and the pain I caused her, my dishonesty, the mural, and the fact that the podcast is back and still hurting people. I pick up my phone, the silence of the group chat echoing through me like a voice in a cave, and I decide to listen to the entire catalog of Tomcat Tea episodes back-to-back, to try and find some clue or pattern I missed before.

Just like I need to make things right with Bree in order to forgive myself for everything that happened last year, I need to figure out who is behind the podcast to get my friends back—to prove to them that I've truly changed.

I won't stop until I've righted all my wrongs.

Oh, look at how the mighty have fallen.

It finally happened. I guess someone other than me knew about Jordyn. And now everyone at school knows the truth. I thought this would feel like retribution, but seeing Jordyn all alone all day was kinda depressing. Made me remember how my cousin felt when things got bad for her—how she was wishing for the days of lockdown when she could just hide out in her room, away from anyone who might be mean to her. But I guess being bullied feels a lot like being called out for the worst stuff you've ever done: It's all shame. And I know from experience that shame is heavy a.f.

She ain't perfect little Jordyn in anyone's eyes now, and I'm happy about that. But I guess I hope she doesn't hate herself.

That's no way to live.

# 16

I'm still listening to Tomcat Tea episodes as I climb onto the bus early the next morning. I got through the whole of the first season last night, and then dreamed in the distorted voice of the podcaster, the cadence and patterns of their speech embedding themselves in my head. I've noticed a few verbal tics they have—clearing their throat in the moments before they drop something heavy, pregnant pauses after certain words, slowing down the closer they get to the end of an episode, the hiccuping sound of their laugh. And in the dream, something about it all felt familiar, like I'd heard those same characteristics in a voice I'd recognize anywhere.

I can't quite place it, so I keep listening, wondering if I'm missing something obvious, something I should be able to put my finger on, like finding a light switch, my hand sliding along a wall in a dark room. But just before I get to school, I switch over to look at Bree's account again. I navigate to the video I bookmarked and watch it in the final stops before it's time for me to get off.

*Hey! So, since I had that one video go viral, I have a bunch of new followers here. I thought it was about time I reintroduce myself, to let all you newbies know who I am and what I'm about. So first, hi again. I'm Bree. As you probably know if you've been here awhile, I was bullied my whole life. It got so bad last school year that I secretly started taking extra classes and signed up for an accelerated program to finish high school over the summer. Unfortunately I didn't make it out unscathed. I had some pretty horrible mental health months, followed by a dark period where I tried to take my own life. During the hardest moments, living felt impossible, but I can honestly say now that I'm grateful to still be here.*

*After that experience, and after I was able to get better with the help of group therapy and balancing my meds, a few of the other kids I met in group who were also victims of bullying and I decided to start a nonprofit. The Bree Project is still new, and we've only visited two schools so far, but we hope to partner with more and speak to elementary and middle school students to address and combat some of the root causes of bullying. I'm glad you're here.*

I replay the video again, then watch a few of her other videos, because Bree seems so different, so much more confident and surer of herself and her place in the world. I'm happy for her. I'm so wrapped up in watching her that I miss my stop and end up having to walk a few extra blocks back to school in the chilly October air, thoughts about the Bree Project spinning in my head.

I still get to school before most of the other students, so I'm able to deliver the portrait letters to each of my friends' lockers without running into them, just like I'd planned. I go to the library, hide in the stacks, and type and retype a message to Bree that I can only hope she'll respond to—a message asking if I can speak to her in person. I finish the homework I didn't get to do last night since I was drawing, and I listen to more Tomcat Tea, feeling a painful kind of hope swelling in my chest—a bubble of air too big for its tiny balloon cage.

It's not even first period yet when it happens. I'm listening to an episode of the podcast when the voice and the person it belongs to clicks into place. I slowly put down the muffin I'm eating, at a table in the back of the library. I don't know how I'm sure, but something in my gut pulsates with certainty. I look through the big window in front of me, imagining the person I now know is behind Tomcat Tea. My heart pounds. My nose and the back of my neck bead with sweat. I look around for Zay, desperate to share this hunch with someone else, to show him the part of the episode that sounds too much like someone we both know, when I see someone else approaching.

As if I've summoned him, Bryce is making his way through the stacks toward me, tripping over his untied laces. He has a small smile on his face and he's carrying the sketch I made for him. I'm unprepared to speak to him so soon after my mind has made the connection between his goofy laugh and the podcaster's, the fact that the pitch is different because of the distortion but that the pregnant pauses and the constant clearing of the podcaster's throat feel too familiar to ignore.

I take him in: the long legs, the thin face, his tousled blond hair. He looks pensive and serious, and I don't want the first words out of my mouth to be an accusation. So I say, "I'm sorry about the election. I know how badly you wanted to win."

He shrugs, like it's no big deal, but I can tell he still cares—that it bothers him he's failed at something his brother was able to do and let his parents down again. But why would he start the podcast, especially if he cares as much as he seems to about what other people think of him?

He puts a heavy hand on my shoulder and says, "Not to be overly earnest on main, but this letter literally made me cry. Maybe because I just lost the election, but reading what you wrote about me really helped me deal with facing everyone today."

I nod, but I feel myself frowning. I look down at my hands.

"Did you make these for everyone else too?" Bryce asks, and I nod again, still unable to say what I'm really thinking. "I figured," Bryce continues. "I don't think anyone else has seen theirs yet, but I'm sure they'll come around when they do."

"That's okay," I say. "I just wanted a chance to tell the truth. So that you all could make your own choices about me with all the information instead of just the sensationalized version of it from the podcast."

I don't think I imagine Bryce averting his eyes.

I swallow hard, then say, "I'm glad you're feeling okay about not winning the election, and I'm sorry if my posters played a role in your loss."

He shakes his head. "Oh, I don't blame you, Jordyn. I had a feeling all along it would be Peyton—everyone loves her."

"She also had a really great speech," I say, wondering if I can annoy him into showing his darker side, a side that could start a podcast like Tomcat Tea. "You told a great story, but she told the truth."

Bryce frowns a little. Pauses like he's thinking, the way he always does. "Damn, Jordyn. That was . . . harsh."

I shrug. "I guess I'm just starting to realize how good you are at making things up. I've never read your stories, but your speech showed that you have a gift when it comes to painting a picture with your words."

Bryce clears his throat. "Wait. What's happening? When I got your sketch and letter, I wanted to find you to say thank you. To say I forgive you for lying. I even texted Zay to see if he knew where you'd be. Why are you being weird?"

My hands shake a little, but then I just say it, let the truth out in a whisper.

"You're the podcaster, aren't you?" I ask, voice low and shaky.

He frowns, chuckles his goofy chuckle, shakes his head. But I notice his Adam's apple move slowly up and down inside his throat, like he's nervous.

Instead of arguing with him, I just stare and ask the one question that's been in my mind for weeks. "Why?"

He doesn't answer. Just says, "Sorry, but you've lost it." He backs away from the table a little, like it's dangerous to be so close to me.

"You didn't get enough attention from the mural? From being on the podcast? You need to have this too?"

"It's not about attention, Bryce. It's about doing what's right. It's about being a good person."

"I *am* a good person. You're the one who ruthlessly bullied your own friend."

Despite my best efforts, him bringing up Bree cuts deep. "You're right. I did. But what do you call what you're doing?" I ask him. "With the podcast? You think your actions are worth admiring?"

"I do," he says, his eyes turning dark. I absently wonder if he realizes that he just admitted what he's done. "Everyone featured on the podcasts is someone who pretended to be one thing when really they're something or someone else behind closed doors. Why shouldn't the world know the truth?"

"You mean like you?" I ask. "Jesus, Bryce. No one is perfect. Doesn't everyone deserve a second chance? Even you?"

He shrugs. "That's just it though. I don't get to mess up. I don't get a second chance at anything."

"What are you talking about?"

Bryce looks around, steps closer to me, and lowers his voice even more.

"I say one wrong thing and Kaleb doesn't feel like I'm a safe friend to come out to. I get one bad grade and my parents chew me out and ask me why I can't be more like my brother. I make a bad joke and suddenly I'm a bad person."

I'm not sure what to say, so I stay quiet, taking in his anger, his frustration, the way he feels so wronged for his own mistakes.

He shrugs. "My parents expected me to win this election. To be just like Cam or better. I'm supposed to be this perfect person, but everyone else can just do whatever with no consequences?" He shakes his head. "Not if I have anything to say about it."

I have no idea what to say or what to think. I blink at him, wondering how long he was planning to keep this up.

"You have to tell Kaleb and Mila and Anton. You have to."

He shakes his head. Crosses his arms. "Why would I do that?"

"If you don't," I warn him, "I'll tell them myself."

Bryce stalks off, leaving me alone with my thoughts, and I'm more confused than ever. I text Zay, *You're not going to believe this,* and ask if I can meet him after school.

———

The rest of the day I wait for Anton or Mila or Kaleb to text me, to come over to me, to tell me they got my apology and that we're okay now. But in class they're still cold and distant, and in the hallways they look away from me, and no one texts. It isn't until the end of the day that my phone buzzes at all. When it does, I reach for it, positive it must be one of my friends. But it isn't.

*I have all your little apology letters*, the text from the private number says. *Don't say a word, or I'll toss these out with tonight's trash. You may have gotten away with threats at your old school, but that's not gonna work here.*

I'm even more confused as to who could be sending these messages, because I put the letters in each of my friends' lockers, but before I text back, I get my answer.

The next message is a photo, and in it I see the bottom hem of khaki chinos, Bryce's untied, well-loved boat shoes. My eyes widen and I slowly reach up to cover my mouth. He has the other sketches. In the photo, he's standing above them and they're spread out, like secrets, at his feet.

# 17

At home, I dive headfirst into my homework, attempting to take my mind off my revelation about Bryce. I start designing the zine, wishing I could send ideas to Kaleb, desperately missing how much we used to text about everything. We had decided before that he would write up the content so I could focus on the look of the zine—pick out the colors, the fonts, figure out the best layout, but now I wonder if he'll want to find a new partner to finish the project with. I try not to think about it, and to pick design elements I think he'd like, with alternates just in case I guess wrong.

Auntie Romy comes into the house as I'm finishing the cover and table of contents, and puts on the kettle. Wordlessly, she makes us both mint tea, muddling fresh mint leaves in deep, heavy-bottomed mugs, and pouring steaming hot water on top. She adds a twist of lemon to each, then leans against the counter and makes a face at me.

"What?" I ask. I'd been looking at my phone, and as I wait for her to answer, I press play on a song we both like. The music rises like the steam from the mugs that sit between us, gently spiraling into the air.

"You're awfully quiet," she says. She squints at me, like if she looks closely enough, she'll be able to see my thoughts. "What's going on with you?"

I swallow hard. Contemplate telling Romy I have a lot of homework and taking my tea to my room. But I lift the mug and blow the steam away, take a sip and it singes my lips.

"I want to tell you something," I say, turning the mug in a slow circle on the counter. "But you can't tell Mom." Romy essentially becomes the eyeballs emoji, then she seals her lips by pulling her pinched thumb and forefinger across her mouth, twisting them against the corner. She throws away an invisible key.

"I know something that could ruin someone. Someone who I thought was a friend. And I can either keep this secret to myself and keep the friend, or tell the truth and lose the friend. I could also lose other friends, if I tell them what I know and I'm wrong or if they don't believe me. But I'd be doing it for the right reasons—this friend is doing something harmful in secret. Does any of this make any sense?"

Romy smiles.

"If what you say is true, and you're doing it for the right reasons, don't worry about who you'll lose. Real friends always come back." I know Romy doesn't have all the details, but in a way her advice feels purer without her knowing exactly what I'm talking about.

"Real friends always come back?" I repeat, and it sounds like a question.

"They do," she says. "Especially when you tell them the truth."

I sip my hot tea, thinking about how the truth can sometimes burn as much as it soothes.

———

Bree responds to my message.

I hadn't been sure if she hated me or not, but her response is warm and open, her reply dotted with emojis and exclamation points. I read it half a dozen times before it sinks in that she isn't angry, that she's open to talking to me, that she's shared her parents' new address.

I shoot her a text before I can talk myself out of it, asking if she's free now. She responds in an instant.

*Yup. I'm here all night.*

When I get to Bree's block in my father's car, I idle on the corner. I take a few deep breaths and shake my hands because the last time I saw her, my old friends were tormenting her while I stood by and did nothing. My heart stutters—a physical reminder that I'm really here. Though I've seen her photos online, in my head I still imagine her as the old Bree. I know it will be unmooring to see her in person after so many long and lonely months.

She looks so happy in her posts, but I'm terrified that everything online is a front, and that she isn't doing as well as her accounts make it seem. I realize I'm more afraid that she's been permanently damaged in some way by my inaction, and that I might get the opposite of closure by coming to see her. Or worse—what if her cheerful message was just a way to bring me here and exact her revenge?

Even though I'm not ready, I take one last deep breath and turn the corner. If I could stand by and let bad things happen, the least I can do now is bear witness to the outcome and try to balance things as best I can with good.

When Bree opens her front door, she's smiling. The first thing I say is "You grew out your bangs" as the tenth-grade version of her— bad haircut, standing in the background in her wrinkled Hartwell uniform and scuffed brown loafers—blends with her now, where she stands in front of me wearing a long floral dress with a denim jacket layered on top. No bangs or bad shoes in sight.

Bree laughs. "Yeah. You can say I've had a mini glow up, I guess." She steps to the side, and invites me in.

"My cousin is visiting; hope you don't mind. You still like tea?" Bree asks, and I feel something that had been drawn tight loosen the tiniest bit in my belly. For all the years we were friends, we really only ever hung out at my house. I don't know Bree's family outside her parents, but the thought of not having to be completely alone with her eases my nerves immediately.

"Yeah, thanks," I tell her.

But when I step farther into her house and turn the corner behind her as she walks into the kitchen, I see someone completely unexpected sitting at the table.

"*Scarlett?*"

"Hey, Jordyn," Scarlett says, like we talk all the time, her laptop open in front of her. Like she hasn't been giving me the evil eye and the cold shoulder since the first day of school.

"Oh, right," Bree calls from the kitchen. "I forgot you guys know each other!"

"I wouldn't say that much," I mutter at the same time as Scarlett says, "*Know* is a strong word."

We look at each other, and her attitude toward me suddenly makes perfect sense. I wasn't imagining things. Scarlett does hate me. Why wouldn't she when I'm part of the reason Bree wanted to die?

"Oh," I say out loud. "You're Bree's cousin." Then I add, stupidly, "But . . . you're Black."

"No duh, Sherlock," Scarlett says, and I hear Bree laugh from the other room.

"Our moms are sisters!" she shouts.

Scarlett looks at me in that dark way of hers, sighs, and closes her laptop. "People don't usually clock the white mom thing because of the whole—" Scarlett gestures at her own face: her brown skin, her short, tightly curling hair, her nose and lips and other features that look so much like mine.

"Right, sorry. That was a weird thing to say. I'm nervous," I admit.

Scarlett shrugs. "It's cool. So, you here to beg for Bree's forgiveness?"

I perch on the edge of the couch. Try to wrap my head around the fact that Scarlett is right beside me, is related to Bree, is speaking to me instead of scowling at me from a distance. I can't stop dissecting the rumors about her and the assumptions I'd made about who she was without ever having spoken to her. How I of all people should have known better than to let the gossip slip into my unconscious judgment of her.

I sigh. "Yeah, basically."

Bree laughs, and Scarlett nods.

Bree brings out the tea and I take a seat on her couch. Scarlett doesn't follow us, but the open layout of the house means she can see us without moving. Bree sits across from me, feet tucked under her in a big blue armchair. She says her parents aren't home, and part of me is glad. I wouldn't want to have to face them yet.

"So, I feel like I should start with an apology," I say after taking my first sip.

"You think?" Scarlett calls, and I grin a little to myself, grateful she's here lightening what could be an impossibly heavy moment. I didn't know she was so sarcastic. I find myself wondering if I could *like* Scarlett, wondering if she could ever like me.

Bree shakes her head. "Ignore her," she says. She cups the mug of tea in her hand, but doesn't drink from it. "I'm listening."

I take a deep and steadying breath.

"I know sorry will never be enough, but I wanted to say it anyway. I need to say it. I need you to know how afraid I was when I came to Hartwell, how angry I was with you for leaving me. I'd known starting over would be hard, but I had never imagined it would be as hard as it actually ended up being. I'm not saying that to excuse my behavior, just letting you know where my head was. That I was scared. That I didn't want to be alone."

Bree's nostrils flare. She sets down her mug on the coffee table between us, her face open and vulnerable as I've ever seen it, and says, "You think *I* wasn't scared? You think *I* wanted to be alone?"

"No, that's not what I'm saying," I begin, but she cuts me off.

"Look, Jordyn. I appreciate you trying to apologize. Honestly. I think it took guts for you to really show up here. I didn't think you would. But I think you should know: The only reason I'm even speaking to you, the reason you're not blocked and the only reason I responded to your DM, is because I know you got expelled for giving Elise a black eye."

I stare at her. "Wait. You know about that?"

Bree kinda laughs a little. "Um, *yeah*. And I know I should be above all that, and that you shouldn't fight fire with fire or whatever. But truly, imagining Elise's face when you came at her, knowing you did come to my defense, however late, got me through some really dark nights."

I bite my lip and cover my face. I glance at Bree from between my fingers. She's smirking. "Oh my God," I say, but then I sober, not wanting to let myself off easy. "I'm glad you know about Elise.

It puts a real action behind what I'm about to say. But I still want to apologize to you."

Bree watches me, her smile fading a little, and gives a small nod. So I continue.

"I'm sorry I let Elise treat you like that. I'm sorry I wasn't there for you when you needed me. And I'm sorry I let it go on for so long. My own fear is no excuse for what I let happen to you. I hope that one day you'll be able to forgive me."

Bree doesn't smile, but she doesn't frown either. Her face remains even, though her eyes look a little glassy.

"Thank you," she says.

"I mean it," I say. "And though I can't speak for anyone else, I hope you know I eventually spoke up for you."

"I mean, yeah," Bree says, picking up her mug again and taking a slow sip. "I bet Elise was sorry after you 'spoke' up for me too."

"Damn right!" Scarlett yells from the dining room.

Bree and I look at each other for only a second before we both laugh.

We spend the rest of the evening catching up, and it's like dipping my feet into cool water after a scorching walk across the pool deck—a shocking, refreshing relief. I tell Bree all about Edgewood, the podcast, and the mural. She tells me about how she spent the summer finishing up what was left of high school, and then she tells me all about the Bree Project, how it started and where she wants to take it next. She says that college classes are tough, but that she loves the freedom of choosing what to learn, and even though she lives at home, she spends lots of time on campus with friends.

We even reminisce about middle school—how we miss being tiny weirdos obsessed with horror movies, dressing in too-big, thrifted clothes, and wearing too much eyeliner, fashion disasters who only loved each other. "I would literally cry when you missed a day of school," I tell Bree.

"I know! I would too!" I'd spent so much time trying to forget about her, forget about our friendship, that it surprises me how easily the warm, gooey feelings come rushing right back.

"You'll find your people in college," she assures me. "I thought you were my only person for so long, but now I know I just needed to put myself out there more, work on liking who I am. And getting a better haircut didn't hurt either."

I smile, but her words make me rethink my whole approach to this year. I've been spending so much time thinking and overthinking my every choice to make sure it was the right one that I forgot how important it is just to be myself. Instead of trying to be the New Jordyn, maybe I need to try harder to be the *real* Jordyn.

"I'm so happy that you're doing so well after everything we put you through," I tell Bree as we stand at the door saying our good-byes. "And I really do want to help however I can with your bullying program. Maybe I can come to one of your speaking engagements and talk to students about how bystanders can be just as damaging as bullies."

"I'll think about it," she says. And while that's usually a gentle way people say no, her smile makes me believe she really will.

Just before Bree closes the door, Scarlett appears beside her. "Since we're all apologizing," Scarlett says, her cheeks a little pink, "I should say sorry too."

"For keeping your distance all semester?" I ask. "For throwing all that shade? You don't need to apologize for that. I get it. You're Bree's family. I more than get it."

"No, not that. I'm . . . actually the reason you were on the podcast before the first day of school," she says.

"Wait. How?"

"I sent in an anonymous tip," she tells me. "Hartwell was required to tell Bree where you ended up attending school the next year to ensure she didn't end up enrolled in the same place. It didn't matter in the end because Bree started college early, but when she found out you'd be going to Edgewood, she told me."

"I mostly told her to make sure she left you alone," Bree cuts in. "I didn't want her harassing you, so I made her promise she wouldn't try to get some kind of revenge."

Scarlett shrugs. "So yeah. Sorry about that."

Completely shocked, I say, "I mean, I guess I deserved it. It's the least I deserved, to be honest." I look at Scarlett and nod, so she knows I don't hold it against her. "I forgive you," I say, and she nods back.

In that moment, I make a decision. I give Scarlett my number. Tell her that there's no pressure, but I'd love to be friends, eventually, if she's open to it.

"I'm not too weird?" Scarlett asks. "Too out there? You're not afraid of all the rumors that might come your way if we hang out?"

I roll my eyes, teasing. "I think I can handle some rumors. I am curious though—why did you leave?" I ask.

Bree speaks up then. "Her dad's in the military. He just got stationed somewhere else. But then her parents got divorced and my aunt wanted to be close to my mom and me." Scarlett throws an arm over her cousin's shoulder.

"We're probably gonna sell our house," Scarlett adds. "The four of us practically live together already."

I smile. I'm jealous. Having a built-in friend like that, who is also your sister-like cousin, has to be amazing. They deserve it. "Bye, guys," I say, feeling choked up and turning to leave before I cry.

When Scarlett waves and says, "See you at school," there's a tiny, not unkind smile on her face.

Hello, listeners! I can't believe we're already five episodes in. I want to start off today's ep by thanking you all again for tuning in and for the support. With that, I know there have been questions about who I am and why I created this podcast. While my identity will remain a mystery, I'm a person who believes in knowing the absolute truth about who you have around you . . .

So many people who go to this school are hiding things or struggling with battles they don't want us to see. If we could all be open with who we really are, it would create the space for people to actually be authentic, rather than surrounded with the superficial and fake BS we're so used to seeing from one another. Whether you're a good person or not, it's time to own up and be you. No matter how uncomfortable that may feel. So if you have a problem with the podcast, you should actually be thanking me. I'm the one bringing the truth to light, so you all can make your own decisions about who you want to be around. Don't they say the truth will set you free?

With that being said, today we're gonna skip the drama and

put the spotlight on our beloved would-be class president, Bryce Green. A few episodes back, I talked so incredibly highly of him, and now . . . it seems he's proved me wrong. Turns out Bryce has a history of being a terrible friend. We all know Kaleb, Bryce's best friend, right? Remember how close they used to be . . . up until a certain incident? Sources tell me Bryce is actually homophobic, and it caused a rift in their friendship. Imagine not accepting not just your friend, but *anyone* for who they really are, free of judgment. And not only that, but coming out is so brave, yet I'm sure incredibly tough . . . imagine leaving your friend to go through that by themselves.

That's not the kind of person I would want to represent us and lead our school. I can wholeheartedly say I will be supporting Peyton, and I hope you do the same. Remember, what happens in the dark always comes to light sooner or later. My job is just to speed up the process. Do with that what you will. Oh, and keep the guessing games of my identity coming, they're fun! Stay messy!

# 18

*"Jordyn Olivia Jones."*

I hear my mother's voice before I see her, stalking down the hall-way toward the bathroom where I'm standing at the sink, brushing my teeth. It's Sunday, and while I'm so relieved about my talk with Bree, I'm still heartbroken about my friends and even more unsure of what to do about Bryce. Now that he's featured himself on Tomcat Tea, I'll look like a liar if I tell anyone that he's behind the podcast. But it's so obvious I want to scream. And now my mom is coming at me, calling me by all three of my names, which means she's pissed. I spit and put my toothbrush away, gripping the edge of the sink to prepare for the impact of whatever she's about to say.

"What the hell is this?" she asks, holding out her phone in my direction.

I take the phone from her. Stare at the *State of the Arts* article with my name right there in the headline: ART AS ACTIVISM: HOW A MURAL BY STUDENT JORDYN JONES CHANGED THE CULTURE AT EDGEWOOD HIGH.

With everything else going on—reconnecting with Bree, my conflict with Bryce, the fight with my friends, and keeping up with school, I'd clearly forgotten to continue worrying about this: my parents discovering the interview where I admit to vandalizing my high school parking lot.

"Oh," I say, feeling like all the air has been sucked out of the room. "I can explain."

She flips her locs behind her shoulder and crosses her arms. When I don't start speaking immediately, she says, "I'm waiting."

"So, there's this podcast," I begin.

"Let me stop you right there. I've read the article. Read several articles about this whole debacle, actually. So I know about the podcast and the gossip and the rumors. I know about Zay and the soccer team and his scholarship. But I also know you know better than to vandalize school property!"

I lick my lips and look down at my bare feet. I'm close to crying but I choke out a "Yes ma'am."

"So why did you do it, Jordyn? Why after everything you

went through last year and this summer would you risk another expulsion?"

I take a deep breath, knowing I only have one chance to make myself understood. I know my mom's patience is running thin, so if she's only going to listen to a few things, they have to be just right.

"This is *nothing* like what happened last year, because I did this for the right reasons. I did this to *stop* harm, to help someone. Zay, yes, but everyone else at Edgewood too."

She squints at me. Looks down at her shoes and sighs. "I believe you," she says. "But that doesn't excuse your behavior. Doing something you know is wrong for the right reasons doesn't automatically make it okay."

"But, Mom." I scoff. "You told me to show everyone who I really am!"

She purses her lips. "Jordyn, please. You know good and well I didn't mean graffitiing your school parking lot. When your father gets home, we'll talk about what your punishment needs to be. For now just go to your room."

My mouth falls open and I want to argue with her, but I can tell by the set of her hips that she's already decided and there's no room for compromise.

I'm annoyed and hurt, and though I'm trying to hide it, I must be doing a bad job.

"You need to fix your face," Mom says. "You're lucky I don't take your phone and everything else away from you right now." I say nothing, head to my room, and push the door closed slowly though I want to slam it behind me.

I wish I could text Kaleb or Mila to complain, but I still don't know where I stand with them. Instead I climb into bed and pull out my sketchbook. I draw it out, as I always do when I feel too many things at once, and what appears before me on the page is a crowd of people, all staring up at the sky, a meteor shower exploding into sparks above their heads, setting parts of the landscape alight as the pieces fall—a fireworks show that seems as chaotic as I feel inside.

I find myself wondering why I'm protecting Bryce, giving him so many chances to come clean on his own, when all he's done this year is hurt other people to protect himself. And I think I figure it out as I draw—Bryce is like the meteor shower, putting on a show no matter what he destroys in the process. But I'm tired of being the reason behind people's pain.

I don't want to hurt him. I don't want to hurt anyone anymore.

But it hurts me that no one seems to see how hard I'm working at everything.

———————

The next morning my parents deliver my sentence over breakfast: I'm grounded. Classes and home and that's it. No phone after 6:00 p.m., and I have to come clean to the administration at school since it seems that they haven't found the article yet.

"I have to turn myself in?" I ask, clarifying that my parents, who were so worried about me doing well and not getting into trouble, want me to essentially volunteer myself for suspension or worse.

"Yep," my dad says, then sips his coffee. "You have to learn to take responsibility for your actions."

"You don't think I know I should take responsibility for the things I've done?" I ask. The frustration of the last week has built a tower inside me, and it's in danger of toppling right over.

I look at them both, but their faces don't seem to show that they get it. And something about that tips me and my tower of feelings over the edge.

"It's like nothing I do is good enough for you," I say. "It's like *I'm* not good enough." And I realize as I say it that this has been my biggest fear: that I'm not good enough. That I can never overcome the past. That no matter how hard I try, I'm not good, period. I grab my backpack and head for the door before the first tear falls, even as I hear my parents calling for me to stop, to listen, that it's not true. Even as the door closes behind me.

———

In first period, Kaleb notices me crying. I try to hide my tears, but my sniffing gives me away. And Kaleb, because he is kind, asks me what's wrong, in spite of everything. "My parents found the *State of the Arts* article, and I'm grounded."

"Oh no," he says. "Tough break." I don't tell him how my chest aches when I think about it. Not because I think the punishment is unfair, but because I'm afraid it means my parents truly don't under-stand why I did what I did. That they really believe there's some part of me that is inherently wrong—some part of me that can't do things right no matter what.

"And . . . I miss you guys," I add tentatively. "I wanted to explain . . . but now everything is a mess and I don't know how to fix it."

Kaleb looks away from me. "Yeah. We miss you too, J. I mean, I miss you. And I feel like our whole friend group is off now, but it's really hard to get past what you did. Have you spoken to Bryce?"

I shake my head, trying to keep my face neutral.

"I'm worried about him," Kaleb continues. "He's been acting

weird and distant ever since he lost the election, and with Tomcat Tea being back, calling him out, I think he's having a hard time too."

I want to tell Kaleb what I know, but Bryce knew what he was doing with this most recent episode of the podcast. He's manipulated everyone so well, and my gut twists when I think of him stealing my apology letters. But I'm not sure telling Kaleb right now is a risk I want to take. I'm so grateful he's talking to me that my heart feels swollen.

I change the subject. "I have to turn myself in today. Part of my 'consequences' according to my parents."

"That's intense," he says.

"I know. I'm a little scared. I'm gonna take the full blame so you don't have to worry about getting into trouble. I won't say a word about you."

Kaleb looks down at his hands and smiles a little bit, but I can't tell what he's thinking.

"Thanks, Jordyn," he says.

---

I head to the office during lunch. After speaking with Kaleb a little bit in class, I attempted to text Mila, and though she gave my message a thumbs-up, she hasn't written back. I plan to look for Anton after I turn myself in—I may just have to try to win my friends back slowly over time, letting my actions speak for themselves since Bryce is holding my apology letters, my literal words, hostage. When I knock on the principal's open office door and he waves me in, I step inside, surprised to see Kaleb sitting there already.

"What are you doing here?" I ask Kaleb.

He looks at me. "You didn't think I'd let you take the fall alone, did you?"

Something syrupy and warm fills my belly, and my eyes sting with the promise of tears. "What?" I say. "Kaleb, you didn't have to—" I pause, unsure of how to finish my sentence. He didn't have to risk punishment just because I am.

Before I can decide what to say, Kaleb is eating up the silence with his voice. "As I was saying, we painted the mural," he says. "We thought it would get the podcaster to chill, but I guess we were wrong. I did the words, Jordyn made it pretty. Sorry."

Kaleb shrugs like he's only admitting to forgetting his home-work. I look from him to Principal Daniels and back again.

Principal Daniels's forehead creases as he frowns. "That true?" he asks. He seems to be addressing the question to me.

I nod, knowing I should be scared or nervous or something, but all I feel is full of something like appreciation, something like love for a friend who wouldn't let me face whatever the consequences of this might be alone. Even if he doesn't know if he can trust me anymore, he's still here for me.

"I'll have to make some phone calls," he says. "Investigate the other leads we had and determine if what you're saying is true. Then I'll need to speak to both your parents and the disciplinary board. You'll be hearing from me or someone else from my office later this week, if not today."

When Kaleb stands up to leave, I wait for him to wink at me or loop his arm through mine, but he doesn't. It's a reminder that we still have things to work through, but then what Romy told me flits through my head: Real friends always come back. And here he is. I just have to be patient.

"Oh my God," I say to him, because I don't think I could tell him thank you without crying. "What were you thinking?"

Kaleb just shrugs again, his hazel eyes shining. He flutters his thick lashes at me, bringing me a step closer to the Kaleb I know and love; the relationship I miss like I'd miss breathing. "What do you think will happen to us?"

"No clue," I say.

But at least we'll be together.

After school I shut myself in the hallway bathroom, sit on the toilet, and call Aunt Romy to tell her about my parents and to give her the news about my in-school suspension combined with Kaleb and me having to paint over the mural. Since we're first-time offenders and didn't actually do any damage to the building itself (thank *God*), we got off pretty easy. I mostly call her to complain, to have someone on my side, but to my surprise, she seems to agree with my parents this time.

"Why is everyone being so hard on me about this?" I ask. "It makes me feel like you're all just waiting for the next time I mess up. Like nothing I do will ever be good enough."

"You may not know this, but it took your parents a long time to get pregnant. And then, when you were born early and so sick, they were so afraid something would happen to you. That's why they've watched you so closely your whole life. It's why your mom wants to have tea with you every day and it's why your dad is so concerned with your schoolwork and your behavior—they put all their hopes and dreams into you."

I pick at a hole in my jeans. "But that's a lot of pressure," I say. "And I'm never going to be able to live up to all that hope. To all those dreams."

Romy makes a sound of disagreement.

"No, you're missing my point. Or maybe I'm not saying it right. *You* are their hopes and dreams. Just you. No matter what you do or where you go. They are always looking out for you, always worried about you, because you are all they ever wanted."

"But I'm always letting them down," I mutter.

"You aren't. And I'll let you in on a little secret. They're being tough on you about this because they knew the school wouldn't be. They'd already spoken to your principal before they sent you to his door. And guess what else?" Romy asks.

I stand up. Look at my wet eyes in the mirror. "What?" I reply.

"They already told me that the mural made them proud."

# 19

Everyone is already in Kaleb's garage when my parents finally say it's okay for me to leave the house again, though I have to be home by seven. The leniency of the school's consequences, along with how I've been going above and beyond all week with chores and homework, has softened my parents' hearts toward me. My stomach is in excited knots the whole time as I rush over. I think I'll be walking into the moment I've been waiting for.

I've begun to tentatively recover some ground with each of my friends, delivering takeout to Mila when she was stuck babysitting, offering to help Anton fill a jar with origami stars for his mom's birthday, joking around with Kaleb again and telling him the truth about my expulsion via a note passed his way during in-school suspension—the first part of our mural punishment.

When I got the text from Bryce to meet everyone here, I assumed he had finally decided to tell the truth. I hadn't heard much from him since I gave him that ultimatum and he threatened me in return, and since Kaleb and I have been stuck in in-school suspension, it's been fairly easy to avoid him at school.

I walk in expecting to see Bryce in tears, or Mila cursing him out, or everyone quietly taking in the news that their friend is the person we've been trying to nail down for months.

But when I knock and the garage door begins to roll back, revealing everyone inside, everything looks calm and normal.

"Hey, New Girl," Anton calls. "You're free! I guess I can't call you that for much longer."

They're all snacking and talking, and music is playing softly in the background. Mila and Anton have their laptops open, while Bryce and Kaleb look like they're doing homework. They all jump up at my arrival, grinning wide, and they all come over and wrap me in a group hug. I stand there slack-jawed for a moment, completely confused.

"Um," I say. "Hi? Bryce, what is going on? You still haven't told them—"

"He gave us your portraits," Mila says. She holds hers up, and then Anton and Kaleb follow suit.

"We're so sorry we didn't listen when you first tried to explain," Kaleb says.

"Yeah. We feel like total assholes. Thank God Bryce passed these along. I'm glad he was more willing to listen than we were."

That's when it clicks. He didn't invite all of us over here to tell the truth. He did it to trap me. To try to convince me to stay quiet by convincing everyone else to give me another shot.

I swallow hard and untangle myself from my friends. My heart pounds at the thought that I could lose this again, that I could lose them again, but this was such a low blow on Bryce's part it's clear he's learned nothing. I can't let it slide.

"It's been over a week, Bryce. I really don't want to be the one to do this."

Everyone looks to Bryce, confused. Bryce looks around at each of us, and part of me is worried he'll lose it, try to turn it all around on me, fight to keep his deception alive. He clearly thought he'd have control over this conversation. That I'd be so grateful to him for helping me get back in the group's good graces that I would help keep his secret. But that's not how this is going to go. "Just tell them," I say.

"Shut up, Jordyn," he says. "The only reason you're even here is because of me. They didn't want you here." His normally well-hidden darkness slips out and around the edges of his words.

"Whoa, whoa, whoa," Kaleb says. "I know we had a rough couple of weeks and everyone is still trying to figure out where we all stand, but Bryce, I want us all to be here. Including Jordyn."

Anton stands up and comes over to where I'm standing. "I want her here too."

Mila says, "Speak for yourself, Bry." And though she doesn't fully assert her allegiance to me, I'll take what I can get.

"Those games you played—they haven't worked," I tell Bryce. I motion to our friends, heart feeling so full that despite everything, they haven't given up on me. "Like I told you before. You can tell them, Bryce, or I will."

Bryce looks like a trapped rabbit. Like he doesn't understand how this could have gotten away from him so completely. He doesn't say anything for so long that I'm about to speak again, when he clears his throat.

"Do you remember how close we were in middle school?" Bryce asks Kaleb.

Kaleb is still frowning when he nods.

"Do you remember why we grew apart?"

Kaleb nods again.

"Mila, do you remember when you started hanging out with us, how I made that one joke you didn't like, and you didn't speak to me for like two weeks?"

Mila looks at me, then back at Bryce. "Yeah, you were being a dick. But we talked about it and it was fine," she says.

"Well, shit like that happens to me all the time. I'm always apologizing. I feel like I can never make a mistake. But everyone else gets away with all the bad stuff that they do and no one even blinks an eye."

"That's not true, Bryce," I say. "I literally got expelled last year."

"You know what I mean. *I* have to be perfect. But no one else does."

I'm tired of waiting for him to get to the point. Tired of listening to his excuses.

"He's the podcaster," I say.

Anton laughs in disbelief. Kaleb keeps frowning. Mila says, "What?" But when Bryce doesn't deny it, when he goes bright red the way he always does when he's embarrassed, our friends' eyes go wide.

"Are you serious?" Mila says.

"No effing way," says Anton.

"That actually makes so much sense," Kaleb says, a tone of awe in his voice. "The way he likes to tell stories. The way the podcaster is always clearing his throat. Wow."

"I can explain," Bryce starts, but Kaleb stands up.

"You need to go," he says. "I can't believe you would do what you did to me, to Mila. To Jordyn!"

Bryce's eyes look glassy. He looks hurt, but so are we.

Anton stands up and presses the button to open the door of the garage. Then he stands there like he's the bouncer at a club. We all watch as Bryce gets his things and slowly walks to the door. Right before he leaves, he turns back, his cheeks blazing.

"This is exactly what I mean," he says, looking each of us in the eye. "Even Jordyn is standing here judging me, when what she did was actually worse. At least I didn't nearly kill somebody. But me? I never get second chances."

She actually showed up.

When my cousin said Jordyn had messaged her, I didn't think she'd really come to Bree's house and apologize. I told Bree F that B, you don't owe her a thing, but my sweet cousin ain't nothing like me. She said, if she doesn't come, then I know. But then she *did*.

I didn't think she'd really help out with the Bree Project either, but she did that too.

I thought I knew how people like her moved. But she keeps surprising me.

I heard she has to paint over the mural now. I guess that was the agreement her parents came to with the school, and if anyone had asked me how I felt about that punishment two weeks ago, I woulda said, "She deserve way more than that."

Now I'm not so sure. Now I'm even thinking about help-ing the girl out.

Funny how quick things, and I guess people, can change.

EPILOGUE

# NOVEMBER

# 20

It's a brisk and sunny morning the first Saturday in November when I get to school with sidewalk chalk and my sketchbook. I arrive way earlier than I asked anyone else to show up, because I wanted to have time to pick which idea of mine would be best to cover up the #secretshurt mural.

I have cheesy sketches, like the one of a bunch of students holding hands or the one of a school bus taking off like a rocket. I have a few serious sketches that illustrate famous graduates and school-spirit-themed ones that highlight some of the school's most successful athletic teams over the years. But the one I like the most, the one I hope Ms. Clayton, the art teacher, approves is a little tongue-in-cheek, which is why I have so many other options.

Ms. Clayton arrives about twenty minutes later, just as I've figured out the best orientation for the new mural that will both obscure the current one and allow for most of it to be seen even when there are lots of cars parked in the lot. She saunters over with her arms crossed, because I've already started sketching the outline of what I want to draw with sidewalk chalk, and she technically hasn't said yes to this particular piece yet.

"Good morning, Ms. Clayton," I say, all smiles. "I know you haven't seen this yet, but I figured I'd get a head start on things just in case it was approved. I thought seeing it laid out like this"—I gesture to the ground—"might help you decide."

She looks down, then takes a few steps back and looks again. "Is that what I think it is, Ms. Jones?" She grins, so I know she gets it.

"Probably," I say. "But to be perfectly clear, here's what I'd like us all to paint today."

I hand her my sketchbook, orienting it the way I want the painting to be on the ground. "Ears up here, feet down by the fence, teacup lifted so that it's closest to that parking space there."

I point and she nods. "Very clever, Jordyn," she says. Then she shakes her head. "It's cute and smart and makes a lot of sense with what this school has been through these past couple of months. I like it."

I smile back. "Then I'll get to work."

I finish up the chalk outline just as the first few volunteers arrive.

Zay shows up looking delicious with most of the soccer team, so I enlist them to carry the paint from the building in shifts and pry open the cans, while the painters work in pairs to finish the mural section by section. When all the colors are open and the work has begun in earnest, Zay kneels and paints beside me. I brush his arm with a stroke of white and he leaves a dot of red on my nose before kissing me in a way that smears the russet paint on his face too. By the time Mila and Kaleb and Anton arrive in the afternoon, a big chunk of it is already done.

"Oh my God," Mila says. Kaleb screams with laughter. And Anton walks around it in a slow circle, snapping progress photos and laughing the whole time. Bryce isn't here, but I think if he'd come, even he might have appreciated what I'd selected as the cover-up mural. Everyone else definitely seems to.

The temperature is dropping by the time we're almost done, so we all pull out mittens and gloves. Ms. Clayton had suggested we do it over the course of two days, but with us being so close to finishing, none of us want to stop. I add one final touch, a swirl of steam twisting across the asphalt as if it's pointing at the school's front door, and then we all step back to admire our work.

Anton races into the building right as the sun starts to set, changing the color of the sky so that we all turn gilded in its glow.

"Golden hour," I whisper, just before I hear Anton's distant voice, yelling.

"Everyone, move back so I can get the full mural before we lose this light!" he screams. We all turn and see that he's on the roof of the school, Frida lifted to his face, his one visible eye screwed shut. Ms. Clayton immediately tells him to get down, but he pretends he can't hear her.

He snaps a dozen photos, then tells us all to crowd around, and he takes a few of us looking right up at him, our heads tilted toward the setting sun. And I feel good. Warm and fuzzy, but also like I'm doing good things again, but this time without the heaviness of shame sitting on my shoulder.

I think that maybe this is how I can try to be good: I can be honest, and real, and do what feels right, even when it's scary. I can be true to myself, and be kind to my friends, and even find sweetness to spare for people who may not offer the same to me. I look over at Scarlett, who I was surprised to see here, and she actually smiles at me. Like Bree, I think she's always been a good person. Not one who is good for show, but someone loyal and real. I think maybe I'm learning how to be good like that too.

Just before we pack up to leave, Bryce walks through the parking lot gate, cheeks reddening as he looks over at us.

I'm surprised to see him approach Scarlett. I wish I could hear their conversation, and I might be imagining things, but from his body language, it almost seems like he might be apologizing, explaining himself, asking for forgiveness. Scarlett's arms are crossed, and I see her roll her eyes a few times, but she doesn't walk away. I hope it is what it seems, and that Scarlett is only the beginning of him making things right with all the people he's wronged.

Because honestly, I don't want to reveal his identity to the entire school. I don't want him to feel the kind of shame that I've carried for so long. I don't want to punish him. I just want him to be done with the podcast for real, to make things right as much as he can, and to never make this kind of mistake again.

Something has been bothering me since he confessed—how he said he never gets second chances. I don't want him to think that's true. I don't want anyone to feel irredeemable. So when he and Scarlett part ways, with her shaking her head like her mind has just been blown, I walk over to him, grab his shoulders, and give him a hug. At first he's stiff and confused, especially because I don't say anything, but slowly he moves to hug me back.

I invite him to come join where our friends are starting to gather, splitting snacks and talking. As we approach, Mila gives him the stink eye, and Anton gives him a wide berth, but Kaleb is the most direct and says, "What you did sucked. If we're ever gonna be friends again, you're going to have a lot of work to do to make things right." Bryce nods, but stays quiet. He seems like he doesn't know what to say.

I want to believe it's possible, to forgive someone but still hold them accountable. To not hold grudges, but to still hold on to the truth. To address toxic behavior without deciding a person is bones-deep bad. I'm not sure if it is, but I think I can give Bryce a second chance even if not all our friends can.

Anton turns his camera around so we can all see the photos he took. They're gorgeous, because Anton is talented and the light is perfect, and my sketch—thanks to a few dozen students and friends—came out exactly the way I'd envisioned it.

Zay comes up behind me then, and says, "Yo, Anton, take one of us." Anton grins and takes a few steps back, lining up the camera so just me and Zay are at the center. He wraps his arms around me from behind, and just before the shutter clicks, he leans down and whispers, "I'm so proud of you." I can't help but smile so wide I show all my teeth.

My favorite photo is the one with all of us in the frame, making funny faces and posing with our pinkies up. Behind us, sprawled across the asphalt, is a huge painting of an orange tomcat assuming the same position, and sipping a cup of steaming-hot tea.

# ACKNOWLEDGMENTS

*Ashley:* Writing a novel is always a bit of a group project, and collaborative novels are even more so! I'd first like to thank Maya and Lexi for asking me to work on this project with them. It was truly a one-of-a-kind experience, and it was so instructive in plot and structure—two things I'm always looking to improve in my writing. I'd like to thank my husband, Cass, for his constant support—you're the best boo and teammate, and I can't imagine doing life without you. Thank you to my agent, Beth Phelan, for her continued diligence and for the humor and compassion with which she handles my neuroticism and anxiety—Beth, you make this work so much easier to do. I can't end these acknowledgments without shouting out to the whole team at Scholastic: Ellie Berger, Leslie Garych, and David Levithan; Elizabeth Whiting, Dan Moser, Jarad Waxman,

Jackie Rubin, Savannah D'Amico, Brigid Martin, Caroline Noll, Melanie Wann, and the rest of the sales team. Thank you to Rachel Feld, Daisy Glasgow, and Greyson Corley in marketing. Thank you to the library marketing team of Lizette Serrano, Emily Heddleson, Maisha Johnson, Meredith Wardell, and Sabrina Montenigro. Thank you to Brooke Shearouse, Seale Ballenger, and Erin Berger in publicity. Special thanks to Janell Harris in production; Jackie Dever, our copyeditor; and Lisa Liu, Jody Corbett, and Jessica White, our proofreaders. Thank you to Steph Yang for the cover design, and thank you to Dr. Tasha Brown for your thoughtful and careful read. It's been a dream, and I hope this isn't the last you'll see of me!

*Lexi:* It has been a dream come true to write this book alongside Ashley. I first want to thank Maya Marlette and Scholastic for the experience of a lifetime and for believing in me every step of the way. Thank you to Ellie Berger, David Levithan, and Leslie Garych for supporting this project. Thank you to our publicist, Brooke Shearouse, and the rest of her team, including Seale Ballenger and Erin Berger. Thank you Daisy Glasgow, Rachel Feld, and Greyson Corley for your amazing IreadYA marketing, and thanks to the library marketing team of Lizette Serrano, Emily Heddleson,

Maisha Johnson, Meredith Wardell, and Sabrina Montenigro. Thank you to the entire sales force for getting this book to readers, including Elizabeth Whiting, Dan Moser, Jarad Waxman, Jackie Rubin, Savannah D'Amico, Brigid Martin, Caroline Noll, and Melanie Wann. Thank you to our amazing sensitivity reader, Dr. Tasha Brown. Thanks to our production editor, Janell Harris; our copyeditor, Jackie Dever; and our proofreaders, Lisa Liu, Jody Corbett, and Jessica White. I never dreamed I would be a published author with the very people who started my love for literature.

I'd also like to thank my mom, Stephanie; my dad, Alex; my nana; and all my family for the constant support—I truly would not be where I am and the person I am today without you. Last but not least, I want to thank my incredible team at CAA and Untitled, especially my literary agent, Cait Hoyt, and my manager, Katie Rhodes. Thank you all for creating space for this audacious visionary to tell stories that I hope will inspire the next generation of YA readers. Forever grateful for the journey.

# ABOUT THE AUTHORS

**Ashley Woodfolk** started reading at age five, writing poetry and stories at age seven, and after majoring in English, worked in children's book publishing for over a decade. Now a full-time mom and writer, Ashley lives in a sunny Brooklyn apartment with her cute husband, her cuter dog, and the cutest kid in the world, and she spends her days (and nights) writing. She is the author of ten books, including *When You Were Everything*, *Blackout*, and *Nothing Burns as Bright as You*. You can find her at ashleywoodfolk.com.

**Lexi Underwood** is an actress, singer, filmmaker, and changemaker. She is best known for her roles in *Little Fires Everywhere*, *Cruel Summer*, *The First Lady*, and *Sneakerella*. In 2018, she founded her production company, Ultimate Dreamer Productions, and made her directorial debut with the docu-short *We the Voices of Gen-Z*. Lexi is committed to using her voice to give back and raise awareness on issues that impact girls and all youth, both locally and globally. Lexi is originally from the greater Washington, DC, area and currently resides in Los Angeles. You can find her online @LexiUnderwood.